Unheard
Voices

Cedar River Daydreams

Other Books by Judy Baer

Unheard Voices

Judy Baer

BETHANY HOUSE PUBLISHERS
MINNEAPOLIS, MINNESOTA 55438

Unheard Voices
Judy Baer

Library of Congress Catalog Card Number 91–77737

ISBN 1–55661–257-5

Published by Bethany House Publishers
A Ministry of Bethany Fellowship, Inc.
6820 Auto Club Road, Minneapolis, Minnesota 55438

Printed in the United States of America

For Laona
with appreciation

JUDY BAER received a B.A. in English and Education from Concordia College in Moorhead, Minnesota. She has had over nineteen novels published and is a member of the National Romance Writers of America, the Society of Children's Book Writers and the National Federation of Press Women.

Two of her novels, *Adrienne* and *Paige*, have been prizewinning bestsellers in the Bethany House SPRINGFLOWER SERIES (for girls 12–15). Both books have been awarded first place for juvenile fiction in the National Federation of Press Women's communications contest.

Give all your worries to him,
because he cares for you.

1 PETER 5:7

Chapter One

Lexi Leighton, Jennifer Golden, and Peggy Madison were quiet as they walked toward Cedar River High School. Only the sound of cars passing and the scuff of Jennifer's leather-soled shoes on the sidewalk broke the silence.

The air was crisp and cool. An early morning frost had left the sidewalks slick, making Lexi feel sure that full-fledged winter could not be far away.

The yards they passed looked sterile, prepared for winter. Gardens had been cleared and cleaned, grass clipped short, leaves raked and bagged, tools and equipment stored.

The sound of Jennifer's shoes against the concrete magnified. "I'm bored," she announced out-of-the-blue. "*Bored. Bored. Bored.*"

"What do you mean by that?" Peggy gestured toward Jennifer's book bag draped over her shoulder. "Not enough homework last night? I had plenty. I could have given you some of mine."

"That's not it. Can't you see?" Jennifer gestured expansively. "Nothing's happening around here. Everything is so predictable. Neat little rows of houses, all painted in earthy hues. Yards trimmed up nicely for the winter.

"And school is even more predictable. Today's Tuesday, right? That means a choice of tuna casserole or chili. Now, *those* are exciting options. On Fridays there's the big question: pizza or lasagna?

"Classes are the same—day after day. Cedar River must be the most boring place on the face of the planet."

"I can't believe you are saying this," Lexi said, shaking her head. "A lot has happened recently. Just since school started this fall, there was Todd's accident . . ."

It still made Lexi shudder to think how close Todd had come to losing the use of his legs. The freak football accident had happened in a matter of seconds, but the pain of his therapy, rehabilitation, and recovery still continued.

"And the changes in youth group," Peggy interrupted. "There's nothing boring about that."

"Right," Lexi agreed. "Ever since Pastor Lake came to Cedar River, things have been happening in the church. Remember all the great new parties and games . . ."

" . . . and the support group for alcoholic teens," Jennifer added. "I know. I know. There have been some things happening."

"My problem this fall should have been enough to keep Cedar River interesting!" Peggy referred to her bout with alcohol abuse. She was in treatment now, but she'd given all her friends, including Jennifer, a bad scare.

"And *Macbeth*! How could you forget the school play?" Lexi chided. "Double double, toil and trouble, caldron boil and caldron bubble," she mimicked Jennifer's lines. "You were one of the best witches ever to cross a stage!"

"And you still say you're bored?" Peggy asked.

"I guess that's *why* I'm bored," Jennifer said. "So many things have happened, that now when it's quiet I'm restless." Jennifer chuckled. "I'll be glad when Todd's on his own two feet again. He snags book bags and turns out lights from halfway across the room with those dumb crutches.

"Even the youth group has settled into a routine," Jennifer continued her complaint. "Business meeting, program, special activities, snack, prayers. You can predict the agenda before you get there."

"The youth group needs structure, Jennifer," Lexi reminded her.

"I suppose so, but it seems to me it's getting a little . . ."

"Boring?" Peggy finished for her.

"Right." Jennifer grinned and stared at Peggy. "Even you've settled down. There's no action anywhere anymore."

"If you call getting well boring, I guess I'm that," Peggy admitted cheerfully.

"You know what I mean," Jennifer said. "The last thing in the world I'd do is criticize someone for regaining control of life. I just wish something different and exciting would happen in Cedar River. Something besides—*algebra*," Jennifer said with a grimace.

Lexi and Peggy both looked puzzled.

"That's right. The most exciting thing in my life right now is algebra—and I hate it. How'd you like to spend every night of the week at the dining room table with an algebra book in front of you?"

If Jennifer expected sympathy from Lexi or Peggy, she didn't get it.

"Excuse me, but did I miss something?" Peggy

said, completely confused. "I don't understand. Why are you taking algebra this year? I took it when I was a freshman."

"Right, and I suppose you think you're smart." Jennifer stuck out her tongue playfully. "Well, I'm stuck in a class with a bunch of freshman, trying to figure out what rational and irrational numbers are. Frankly, I think the whole crazy system stinks!"

"Seriously, Jen," Lexi interrupted. "Why are you taking first-year algebra now? I took it when I was a ninth-grader at Grover's Point."

"Why do you think, Lexi?" Jennifer said evenly. "Because I'm *dyslexic*."

"Does that affect your algebra, too?" Peggy asked.

"Yes. I've managed to put it off until now because I knew it would drive me crazy. Numbers are scrambled on the page for me just like letters are. And letters *and* numbers put together in formulas drive me absolutely bonkers."

"Oooooooh," Peggy intoned sympathetically. "That's rough."

"I thought I could somehow slip through high school without anyone noticing the fact that I hadn't taken algebra," Jennifer admitted. "Boy, was I wrong."

"Who picked up on it?" Lexi asked.

"The math teacher, Mr. Stewart. He's my advisor this year, and he says I shouldn't put it off any longer—I have to take it. I begged, of course, but he said there was no alternative."

"Bummer!" Peggy empathized.

"I feel like a real dummy sitting in a class with freshmen, but I have no choice. It's really getting me down, though. I felt like it was a major accomplishment getting through my sophomore year. Having a second-hour class with *freshmen* sort of makes me feel like I'm backtracking."

"There are a lot of nice people in that class." Lexi tried to sound encouraging.

"It's not really the students that I mind. It's just that they're younger, and they get the math. I don't understand it, Lexi. It doesn't make any sense to me."

"How come you've never mentioned this before? We didn't even realize you were taking the class," Peggy repeated.

"I was hoping I could get through it without making a big production of it. I was embarrassed, I guess. I muddled along through the easier part, but now we're doing factoring and Mr. Stewart is talking about quadratic equations. I can't even spell it! There's no way I'm going to figure it out." Jennifer kicked at some loose stones. "Sometimes I feel so stupid."

"You're not stupid!" Lexi insisted. "You're one of the smartest girls I know. You have a learning disability. That doesn't make you stupid."

"It makes me *feel* stupid," Jennifer retorted. "Why can't I learn this stuff?" There was despair in her voice.

Lexi knew how hard Jennifer worked in school. She also knew how difficult it was for Jennifer to master things that others took for granted.

"Don't let it get you down," Lexi advised. "Why not treat algebra like . . . like a foreign language!"

"It *is* a foreign language," Jennifer moped. "And I don't want to learn another language. I have enough trouble with English. My life is just not any fun. I guess that's why I'm bored."

The girls had arrived at the school. Lexi pulled open the heavy metal door and allowed Peggy and Jennifer to enter ahead of her. The hall walls had been painted over the weekend, and the smell of fresh paint greeted them. "Ugh," Jennifer groaned.

The usual chaos of students digging books from their lockers, calling to friends, and pushing their way to classes was all around them.

"Excuse me. Excuse me. Excuse me," Lexi said mechanically as she made her way toward her own locker. She'd emptied her book bag and taken up books for the first hour, when Tim Anders called to her.

"Hey, Lexi. When will Todd be coming?"

Lexi closed her locker and secured the books in the crook of her arm. "He'll be here sometime after the second bell."

"But, he'll be late for school."

"If he comes on time he's got to maneuver through the crowd. With study period first hour for him, it doesn't really matter if he's a few minutes late. It seems to be working out best that way."

"I'm glad he's back." Tim smiled at Lexi. "Todd's really a great guy."

"I think so, too. School just wasn't the same when he was in the hospital."

Lexi stared thoughtfully after Tim as he left. In a way, Jennifer was right. School *was* a little boring. While Todd had been in the hospital, there'd been plenty to think and worry about. Now he was back and doing well. When the school production of *Macbeth* closed, things had quieted down even more—maybe a little too much.

Lexi shook herself. *What am I thinking? My life has been jam-packed with excitement over the past months. I should be grateful for a little peace and quiet!*

The peace and quiet didn't last long. Binky McNaughton raced down the hall toward Lexi as fast as her skinny bird-like legs would carry her. Her eyes were sparkling. "Have you seen her?" Binky gasped breathlessly.

"Seen who?"

"The new girl, of course."

"What new girl, Binky?"

Binky was bubbling over with excitement. "There's a new girl enrolling at Cedar River today. Egg and I saw her go into the administration office with her parents. We stood around a few minutes waiting for her to come out, but she hasn't yet."

"Did everyone get this excited when I started school here?" Lexi asked. "Did you stand outside the office waiting to get a glimpse of me?"

Binky looked exasperated. "Of course not, Lexi. You were interesting. Don't get me wrong. But this girl, well, she's . . . unique."

Lexi tried to imagine what would make the new girl "unique" enough to cause this kind of excitement. "What was she doing? Walking on her hands; leading a dancing bear?"

"Oh, Lexi. You're too much." Binky shook her head and smiled halfheartedly. "Wait till you see her. Then you'll understand."

Chapter Two

"I don't see what all the excitement is about," Lexi said. "New families move into town all the time. Surely there's nothing so unusual about one more new student!"

"Not usually," Binky agreed. "But everyone's wondering what's wrong with this one."

"Binky! The poor girl has been in the school fifteen minutes and already you think something's *wrong* with her? I hate to think what they said about *me* the day I arrived."

"Oh, nothing, Lexi. You were . . . that is, you looked . . . normal. This girl is very . . ." Binky paused, searching for the right word. ". . . different."

"Different? What do you mean, Binky? No one could be more different-looking than your brother Egg, for example."

Binky chuckled. It didn't sound like an observation Lexi would make, but it was funny just the same. "You don't understand, Lexi. You're not listening to me!"

"All right." Lexi paused in the hallway. "Tell me what it is you're trying to say."

"The new girl looks different because she wears these . . . things . . . on her ears."

"What kind of things?"

Binky didn't answer because they'd arrived at their classroom door. A girl unfamiliar to Lexi stood next to Mr. Raddis's desk.

"There she is!" Binky whispered. "See what I mean?"

The new girl looked shy and unsure of herself. Lexi noticed what Binky had been referring to. It was obvious the girl wore hearing aids on both ears.

"Have you ever seen such huge hearing aids?" Binky whispered as they slid into two desks near the window.

"No. I guess they show more because she wears her hair pulled back."

"I wonder why she doesn't wear the little ones that fit inside your ears?"

"Maybe she doesn't have any choice."

Lexi tried in vain not to stare at the girl. Her hair was plain brown, and she had a smattering of freckles across the bridge of her nose. Her lips were pressed tightly together, and she looked nervous and bewildered. Actually, she was very sweet-looking, Lexi decided, but also appeared to be terribly frightened.

The new girl's most attractive feature was her eyes. They were big and blue, and she had long, dark lashes. But her gaze darted from side to side as if she were wary of everyone in the room.

"She's thin, isn't she?" Binky whispered over Lexi's shoulder. The girl was slender, definitely not the athletic type.

Her clothes were loose fitting, neat and clean, but simple. Lexi couldn't help thinking she could make the girl look more attractive if she could take some darts and tucks in the garments to make her clothes fit better.

Lexi's mother had always taught her that it wasn't *what* a person wore, but rather *how* they wore it that made the difference.

Lexi noticed she was not the only one staring. Nearly two dozen pairs of eyes were fixed on the newest member of the class. The girl was obviously aware that she was the object of everyone's attention. She smiled tentatively around the room.

Mr. Raddis looked up from the papers he'd been examining and tapped his pencil on the desk. "Attention, please. I'd like to introduce a new member of our class. This is Ruth Miller, recently moved to Cedar River from Boston."

It seemed to Lexi that Mr. Raddis was speaking louder than usual. "I hope you'll all welcome her to our school. Ruth, would you like to say something?"

"No, thank you," the girl said politely. Her voice sounded flat.

"Why does she sound like that?" Binky mouthed as Mr. Raddis directed Ruth to a seat on the far side of the room.

"Because of her hearing handicap, I suppose," Lexi whispered back.

"Oh. I get it." Binky turned back to her books.

The class proceeded without incident, and before Lexi could think anymore about the shy new girl, it was time for lunch.

The entire gang was gathered at one table. Matt and Todd were deep in conversation about cars and motorcycles. Peggy, Jennifer, Binky, and Anna Marie were being entertained by Egg, who was attempting to balance spoons on his nose.

The floor was littered with fallen silverware. Lexi was surprised the cafeteria monitors hadn't put a stop to his comedy act.

"Oh, Egg, give it up," Lexi teased as she brushed past him to join the others. "You'd better pick up those spoons before you get caught."

"How am I supposed to learn to perform before an audience if I keep getting interrupted?" Egg asked grumpily.

"Is that your goal? To be a juggler?"

"Who knows. I got a terrible grade on my science test; I'll probably never get into college." He blew on the bowl of a spoon and balanced it once more on his nose. "Do you think there's any room for my talent in the entertainment world?"

The conversation turned to speculation on where Egg could demonstrate his new routine.

Lexi ignored the comments as she watched the line of students coming through the cafeteria. Ruth Miller walked in alone, avoiding conversation with anyone.

Lexi wondered if the girl was able to hear all the ruckus that was going on around her. She thought back to her own first day at Cedar River. It had been very difficult to walk into the huge cafeteria, alone and unsure of herself.

Ruth made her way to an empty table near the doorway, away from the hubbub. Lexi ached for her. She knew exactly what it felt like to be the new girl in school.

Lexi decided that as soon as she was finished eating she would go and speak to Ruth. But just as she stacked her dishes on the tray, she noticed Minda Hannaford sauntering toward Ruth's table. Minda looked to Lexi like a wild cat stalking its prey. Minda slid into the seat across from Ruth and began talking loudly.

Lexi could tell, even from across the room, that Minda was drilling Ruth with questions. She also knew from the pained expression on her face that Ruth wasn't doing too well answering them. Perhaps she wasn't able to understand Minda's rapid-fire manner of speaking.

"Move over, Egg," Lexi murmured. "I want to get up."

"Where are you going?" Egg asked. "I've got another joke to tell."

"I'll hear it later," Lexi promised, trying to leave without causing a scene.

"I'm going to get a complex if you don't listen to my jokes, Lexi."

Lexi felt the exasperation rising within her as she saw Minda stand up, toss her long hair over her shoulder, and leave Ruth's table. Ruth's head was bowed, a picture of dejection. Before Lexi could reach her, she'd left the cafeteria.

What had Minda said to Ruth to make her leave so suddenly?

Chapter Three

"Don't you feel just awful for that new girl?" Jennifer's features showed real concern. "I've never seen another human being look so absolutely miserable. I tried to talk to her after school, but when I approached her, she darted away."

"She did look pretty nervous," Egg agreed. He and Todd had joined Jennifer, Peggy, and Binky at Lexi's house to do some homework.

"Who wouldn't be scared after getting the third degree from Minda Hannaford?" Binky chimed. "Everyone saw her talking to Ruth at lunch. It was obvious it didn't take Minda long to decide Ruth wasn't her type."

"You're being awfully hard on Minda," Lexi said. "Maybe Minda was trying to be friendly."

The others all stared at Lexi in disbelief.

"I can't believe you said that," Binky remarked.

"We all know Minda well enough to know she wasn't just trying to be friendly," Todd pointed out. "But I don't think Minda realizes the effect she has on people, though." He whistled between his teeth. "She even scares *me* sometimes!"

"All I'm saying is that we don't know what Minda said to Ruth," Lexi explained. "Maybe she was being more friendly than we give her credit for."

Egg was sprawled on the floor feeding himself red licorice. "Maybe Lexi's right."

"Lexi, you always look for the best in people," Binky said, searching for cashews in the bowl of nuts on the coffee table. "No matter what Minda said, we should be friendly to Ruth. She's going to have a hard time adjusting to school. Having a hearing disability is bad enough, but having Minda on your case . . . well . . ."

Todd groaned and punched his fist at the book in front of him. "Is everyone done with their history?"

"I am," Lexi answered.

"I'm stuck on question fifteen," Jennifer admitted.

"I forgot to bring my book home," Egg said, looking sheepish.

"Me too," Binky added.

"Oh, well." Todd nudged the book shut with the tip of his pencil. "It can wait until tomorrow. I don't feel much like doing homework now anyway."

"*You* don't feel like doing homework?" Jennifer glared at her algebra book. "How do you think *I* feel? Can anyone here help me with the division of exponents?"

"Do both numbers have the same base?" Egg asked.

"I guess so."

"Then subtract the exponent in the denominator from the exponent in the numerator. Then you can raise the base to the resulting exponent."

"Huh?" Jennifer stared at him blankly. Egg scrambled to his feet like a spider.

"Here. Let me show you. Have you got any scratch

paper?" He sauntered to the table where Jennifer was working and leaned over her shoulder. "It's easy, really. See? You have X to the ninth, divided by X to the sixth. That equals X to the ninth minus six. Nine minus six is three. That means the answer is X to the third."

"Right, Egg. It's perfectly clear now. Clear as mud. Here, show me again." Jennifer thrust a notebook at him.

Lexi watched Egg and Jennifer a moment, then turned to Peggy, who was sitting silently in a corner of the room. She'd been so quiet, Lexi had almost forgotten she was there.

Her hands were folded in her lap, her eyes closed. Lexi realized Peggy hadn't said a word since they'd arrived.

"What are you thinking about, Peggy?"

"I'm trying to imagine what it must be like to be deaf," Peggy said. She squeezed her eyes even more tightly shut. "But I can't seem to do it."

"It looks like you're trying to imagine being blind," Todd pointed out.

Peggy's eyelids fluttered open. "Oh, you're right. I should have my ears plugged." She clapped her hands over her ears. "No matter what I do, I can't shut you out."

"That's 'cause we're a noisy bunch," Binky said.

"Even with my eyes closed, trying to ignore the sounds, I could hear almost everything," Peggy said thoughtfully. "For instance, I knew Egg was eating licorice."

"What about me?" Binky asked mischievously.

"You're eating nuts," Peggy said. "Knowing you, probably the cashews."

Binky's mouth dropped open. "I'm that predictable, huh?"

"And with my hands over my ears, I still know what's going on in the room. I can't shut out all the sound. That would be awful. Even though I could see everything you're doing, to not hear all of you would make me feel cut off from you."

"So what's worse then? To be blind or deaf?" Binky wondered aloud.

"Both would be awful," Peggy concluded. "But I think being deaf would make you feel more lonely."

Lexi thought of Ruth Miller sitting alone in the cafeteria. Then she remembered the sound of her flat, toneless voice. There was no doubt Peggy was right. Being deaf would be a very lonely existence. Lexi had had a difficult time becoming acquainted at Cedar River when she first arrived, *without* any handicaps.

"Tomorrow we should all make a point of telling Ruth we're glad she's moved to Cedar River," Lexi said with conviction. "And we should smile at her when we see her in the hall—let her know she's welcome."

"I can do that," Egg said, chewing thoughtfully on another piece of licorice. "But she hardly ever looks up. She won't see our smiling faces."

"I heard some junior high boys teasing Ruth while she waited outside the school for her ride home," Peggy said. "They asked her questions about her hearing aids. When she answered them, they made fun of her speech." Peggy shuddered. "It was awful. They were pretty cruel. I hope Ruth didn't understand everything they said."

"Someone should invent a hearing aid that filters out all the bad stuff," Binky said. "Wouldn't that be great?"

Egg had seated himself crosslegged on the floor. He held his hands over his ears and stared at the wall. "Say something to me," he ordered.

"Egg, you're one of a kind," Todd obliged cheerfully.

"Not so loud. Talk in your normal voice. I could hear that."

"Egg, you're a nut," Todd said more softly.

"Did you say, 'Egg, you're a mutt'?" Egg asked.

"No, I said you were a nut."

"Oh." Egg looked puzzled. "Not hearing well can distort simple words."

"It certainly can," Binky agreed. "Wouldn't you like to know what Todd really called you?"

Egg ignored his sister. He was obviously intent on learning more about the hearing-impaired. He scrambled to his feet and moved toward the television set. He turned it on, adjusted the volume to low, and pulled up a footstool.

"What are you doing now?" Binky asked sharply.

He waved a hand without turning his head. "I'm trying to get the gist of this program."

"Then why don't you turn up the volume? It's hard to understand without the words."

"I know," Egg muttered. "That's the idea."

"Oh, I get it." Binky dragged her beanbag pillow toward Egg. "You're trying to imagine what it's like to have Ruth's problem."

"Be quiet," Egg hissed. "It isn't easy to figure out the story line when you can't hear the words."

Egg's comment drew the others to the television screen. Soon they were all staring intently, straining at the sound of voices they couldn't quite make out.

It was onto this unusual scene that Lexi's father

entered. He stared at Lexi and her friends. "What's going on?"

Binky squeaked in surprise. "Oh, Dr. Leighton! You startled us."

Lexi reluctantly looked away from the television. "We're trying to figure out the plot of this story."

"Wouldn't that be easier with the volume up?"

"There's a new girl at school, Dad. She's deaf. We were trying to imagine what it must be like for her." Lexi glanced ruefully at the screen. "When the words aren't clear, the actors look like so many fish gaping at you through aquarium glass."

Egg turned the volume up slightly.

"Oh, that's better," Jennifer said.

Todd massaged the muscles at the back of his neck. "Much better. I didn't realize how tense I'd become trying to figure out what those people were saying."

"Think about Ruth." Binky sounded very sympathetic, and looked as though she were about to dissolve into tears. "There's no way she can turn up the sound."

"I thought it would be easier to read lips," Jennifer admitted. "But there's no way I could do it. I suppose I could get used to lipreading the same person all the time, but it would be hard to learn to lipread a person I'd never met before."

"I'd hate to be deaf," Binky said. "You'd be shut off from everything and everyone. Even with the hearing aids, Ruth doesn't seem to understand everything that's said. Not hearing a person's tone of voice would mean you'd never know if they were angry or sad, happy or giddy."

Dr. Leighton listened to the conversation with an amused look on his face.

"What're you thinking, Dad?" Lexi asked.

"Oh, nothing. I just marvel at how you young people get so vitally interested in something and then try to figure it out."

"We don't know much about deafness, I guess," Lexi said forlornly.

"You're a doctor!" Egg piped up. "A veterinarian must know something about deafness."

"I know a little." Dr. Leighton sat down. "I can tell you how the ear works. The outer ear is a collector. It gathers vibrations, or sounds, that travel through the ear canal to the eardrum. When the sound waves hit the drum it vibrates. From there the sounds are passed to the inner ear where they become electrical signals that the auditory nerve carries to the brain, where they are deciphered.

"The ear is a marvelous instrument that most of us take for granted."

Binky still looked a little confused.

"Binky, would you like to feel some sound?" Dr. Leighton asked.

"Huh?"

"Put your hand on your throat and make a noise."

Binky held her fingers to her throat and made a humming sound. "My throat is moving all right."

"Exactly. You're making your vocal cords vibrate. That sound travels along the auditory nerve in the ear and the brain interprets it."

"Do you know what causes deafness, Dr. Leighton?" Todd asked.

"There are many causes. Some people are born deaf. Sometimes it is caused by accident or disease, affecting the small bones in the ear—the stirrup, the anvil, or the hammer. Infections can scar the eardrum and cause damage. Even extremely loud music can do a great deal of harm to a person's hearing."

Binky's eyes grew wide. "I wonder what happened to Ruth."

"We don't know, but we're sure lucky, aren't we?" Lexi said. "We can hear."

"Very lucky." Binky nodded.

Just then, Lexi's little brother Ben bolted into the living room waving a piece of paper. "Look! Look! See what Ben's got!" He waved an envelope high over his head.

Lexi reached out for it, but Ben darted out of her reach.

"What have you got, Ben?" Egg asked. "A love letter from your girlfriend?"

Ben made a face.

"Is it a note from your teacher at the Academy?"

"You're teasing me." Ben drew the paper close to his chest and crossed his hands over it.

"I won't tease you, Ben. Let me see the note," Lexi cajoled.

"Guess," Ben demanded. "Guess what it says."

"You inherited a million dollars!" Todd joked.

"No, Todd. You're silly."

"You have to stay after school every night this week," Jennifer offered.

Ben guffawed loudly at that suggestion. "Guess who it's from."

"Your mom," Jennifer said.

"That little girl you have a crush on at school," Egg insisted.

"Wrong!" Ben announced. "It's from Pastor Lake."

"When did you get a note from Pastor Lake, Benjamin?" Lexi asked.

"It came in the mail. Mom gave it to me today." Ben handed the letter over to Lexi. "Gotta go. Bye!" Benjamin dashed out of the room.

Lexi opened the envelope and scanned the letter. "It's the teen newsletter from church. It gives the date of the overnight retreat."

"Retreat? What retreat?" Peggy asked.

"You and Todd weren't at the last meeting," Egg acknowledged. "The youth group decided to have a retreat. Pastor Lake said he'd make the arrangements and let us know when something was settled."

"It will be the first ever. Isn't that great?" Binky's eyes twinkled with excitement.

"Where is it going to be held?" Todd asked.

"At a Bible camp fifty miles from here," Lexi said, still scanning the newsletter for more information. According to this, we'll have the entire retreat center to ourselves."

"Great!" Egg enthused.

"Several stores and restaurants have offered to donate food for our meals—like pizza and stuff."

"All right!" Egg cheered. "I'm going!"

Binky fell back on the couch and thrust her legs into the air. "I can hardly wait."

"Sounds good to me," Jennifer said nonchalantly.

"Well, sounds like you have some plans to make." Dr. Leighton rose from his chair. "If you'll excuse me, I think I'll go find Ben."

"See you later, Dad."

"Will we need to bring sleeping bags?" Jennifer asked.

"I wonder if they have electricity," Peggy worried.

"I'll need to plug in my curling iron."

"Food. We'll need lots of it. The pizza won't last long. Maybe I could bring some food in my suitcase." Egg dug in his pocket for a scrap of paper. "I'd better make a list of what we'll need . . ."

"Do you think they'll take a guy like me?" Todd questioned. "I mean, with the crutches and all."

"Do you think they'll take girls who are flunking algebra?" Jennifer asked.

In the animated discussion and excitement of the upcoming retreat, no more mention was made of Ruth Miller.

Chapter Four

Lexi looked up from her homework to see Jennifer staring cross-eyed at her from across the table. "Algebra problems?"

Jennifer ran her fingers through her hair until it stood on end. "I'm going to get through this. I *have* to. The problem is *how*. Lexi, every time I walk into the classroom I panic. It's like my stomach is on a roller coaster, and after a steep drop-off, it sinks to my feet and stays there until the bell rings. What am I going to do?"

"You're panicking before the class even starts, Jennifer. Maybe that's why you aren't understanding it."

"Could be," Jennifer agreed morosely. "I have this terrible fear of making a fool of myself. I've done it enough times. I should be used to it by now, but I'm not."

"You've convinced yourself that you're going to flunk algebra. You aren't giving the class a chance."

"But none of it makes sense to me, Lexi. And I can't help that."

"What do you do when you are confused by the material?" Lexi asked.

"Usually I close my book, shut my eyes, and wait

for class to be over. My brain screams *overload* and stops functioning."

"You're psyching yourself up for failure, Jennifer. You're so sure you can't do algebra that you're not even trying."

"But what about my dyslexia?"

"You've learned to work through it in other classes. Why can't you do the same in algebra?"

"Maybe I can," Jennifer murmured doubtfully.

"You need to keep a positive attitude," Lexi encouraged. "After all, you do have to pass algebra in order to graduate from high school."

"That's the reason I'm panicking."

"Maybe you could get someone to help you—like a tutor."

"Who's good at algebra who would have time to help me?" Jennifer moaned. "I know Todd's good, but he's got a lot on his mind trying to get caught up on his homework, plus the physical therapy."

"I'd help you," Lexi offered, "but algebra is not my strong point. Maybe if your attitude changed, your teacher would see that you're making an effort and give you a break."

"Speaking of teachers, how do you like Mr. Oakley, the new computer instructor?"

Lexi wrinkled her nose. If algebra was Jennifer's big roadblock, the computer was hers. "He's okay, I guess."

"Just *okay*?"

"Actually, he's not my favorite teacher. He's very impatient. If someone doesn't understand his instructions the first time, he yells at the person."

"That does a lot of good," Jennifer said sarcastically.

"Yeah, really. He actually shouts at students who don't catch on. He talks very fast and is hard to understand. Besides, I don't like his moustache. It's so bushy and droopy—like he's trying to hide his mouth or something."

"I'm taking the computer course next semester. I don't anticipate any trouble, because I really like computers," Jennifer explained. "I just don't need another course like algebra."

Lexi adjusted her backpack for the walk home after school the next day. The air was cool and there was a brisk wind. The school buses had already left and the parking lot was nearly empty.

As she headed down the street, she noticed a girl walking ahead of her that she didn't recognize. As she got closer, she realized who it was.

"Ruth! Wait up. Ruth!"

The girl continued to walk quickly and methodically.

"Ruth! Wait, I'll walk with you!"

No response.

Lexi called louder, which drew a perturbed expression from a man who was filling a bird feeder in his yard. Finally Ruth paused and turned around hesitantly. It was obvious that she was surprised anyone would call after her.

Lexi was out of breath by the time she reached Ruth. "You're a fast walker. I've been trying to catch up with you for a block and a half."

Ruth looked puzzled. "Why?"

"Because I wanted to walk with you," Lexi said.

"But why?"

It was hard for Lexi to contain a smile.

"Because I was walking alone and you were walking alone. I thought it would be fun to walk together and get to know each other."

Ruth digested the bit of information and replied solemnly, "Oh."

"I know you're new at school. I moved to Cedar River just over a year ago, and I know what it's like to be the new girl in town."

Ruth nodded.

"It's difficult to lose old friends and to make new ones," Lexi empathized. Ruth's silence was beginning to make Lexi feel uneasy. "When did you move to Cedar River?"

"Last weekend."

"Oh. You're really new here then, aren't you." Lexi looked right at the girl and smiled broadly.

The corners of Ruth's mouth quivered slightly.

"I moved here from Grover's Point. Have you heard of that town?" Lexi tried not to be discouraged by Ruth's lack of enthusiasm.

"No."

"Ummm, uh," Lexi stammered. "Maybe you wanted to walk alone. I'm sorry if I intruded."

Ruth's eyes lit up with alarm. "Oh no. Please stay." A pink blush rose in her cheeks. "I'm glad you caught up with me."

"Maybe you'd rather not talk," Lexi ventured.

Ruth looked down. "I'm embarrassed to talk. I know my voice sounds funny."

Lexi had hardly noticed this time. "Oh, you sound fine," Lexi assured her. "Where do you come from, Ruth?"

"We were in Boston last."

"I've heard that's a beautiful city. Did you like it there?"

"We weren't there very long," Ruth admitted. "Only a few weeks."

"Then you moved here?"

"I suppose I should explain." Ruth's voice was clear but without expression.

"My parents are missionaries. They work overseas."

"Missionaries? That's great! What's it like to be a missionary kid?"

"Good . . . and not so good. We've traveled a lot. That's exciting. I've seen many parts of the world, but I've also been left behind for school a lot. That's the hard part."

"I'll bet. I'd hate to be away from my parents for long periods of time. Especially if I couldn't call them whenever I wanted to."

"I write a lot of letters, but it's not the same." Ruth smiled a little. "When they come home they talk about all the things that have changed since they left the country. Going into some parts of the world is like stepping into a time warp. When they come back it takes a while to catch up again."

"What do you think of Cedar River? The school, I mean."

"It's all right. I've met some nice people . . ."

And some not so nice, Lexi thought.

"It's pretty here," Ruth continued. "The school is bigger than I'm used to, but I suppose I'll adjust."

"I did," Lexi consoled. "Just give it time."

"My aunt lives in Cedar River. I'm going to stay with her until my parents are settled. Then they might send for me." Her expression turned wistful. "It could be a long time."

"Then you'll join them on the field?"

"It all depends on whether they find a good school there. They worry about me because of my hearing loss. They don't want me to fall behind in school." Ruth sighed. "I'm glad my classes aren't all like the computer class." A faint smile touched her lips. "I'd do better if Mr. Oakley would trim his moustache. At least then I could read his lips."

"Well, if it's any consolation," Lexi added with a smile, "I'm not doing so well in that class, either."

Lexi felt sorry for Ruth, having had to say goodbye to her parents, adjusting to a new school, and coping with a hearing impairment at the same time.

"Did your parents leave recently?" Lexi asked.

"Just yesterday." Ruth's eyes glazed with tears. "I miss them already. I told myself I wouldn't get emotional this time, but I can't help it. My aunt is nice, but it's not the same as having my parents around."

Lexi remained silent until they reached her street.

"Well, I suppose I'll see you in Oakley's class tomorrow," Lexi said cheerily.

"Yes. And thanks . . . you know . . . for walking with me and everything."

———

The next morning, Lexi thought about the conversations she'd had with Jennifer and Ruth. As she walked down the hall to her computer class, she felt a knot tighten in her stomach. Lexi had always liked school, but she didn't enjoy the feeling she had when she entered Mr. Oakley's classroom.

"Are you ready for this?" Binky whispered as she came up beside Lexi.

"I don't think I'll ever be ready." Lexi dreaded the class more than any other. But she'd given Jennifer a pep talk about having a good attitude. Now she needed to work on her *own* attitude toward Mr. Oakley and computers.

"Look where that new girl is sitting," Binky murmured.

Ruth Miller was seated on the far side of the room behind the computer everyone called "the clunker," so named because it was the poorest computer in class. Everyone came early in order to avoid having to use it.

"Why is she sitting there?" Binky questioned. "That's a terrible computer. It's slow and the screen is almost impossible to read. I had to work at it one day last week. Half the screen fades out so you can't see what you're doing."

"Maybe no one told her about the clunker." Lexi wished she'd thought to warn her new friend.

"Everyone in your places, please. No more dawdling." Mr. Oakley spoke sharply from the front of the room.

Lexi and Binky scurried to their seats.

In his quick, staccato delivery, Mr. Oakley spat out instructions for the day's project. While all the other students began to work, Ruth remained still. She obviously hadn't caught all Mr. Oakley had said.

To make matters worse, the teacher turned his back toward the class and gave more instructions while writing on the blackboard. His voice was muffled even to Lexi's ears. Mr. Oakley often turned away from the class while he was speaking. Though most class members could probably hear him, the look of confusion on Ruth's face was heartbreaking.

Mr. Oakley turned to face the room. "You have all the instructions you need to complete this project. It's going to take the full hour, so don't waste any time. Load your machines and get going."

Ruth sat with her hands folded in her lap waiting patiently. After a few agonizing minutes, Ruth raised her hand.

"Yes? What is it?" Mr. Oakley's tone was cold.

"May I have some help with this computer? I don't understand . . ." Ruth's voice was flat, expressionless.

"Oh, you're the new girl. I believe I asked you to bring some papers with you to class. I hope you left them on my desk; I'll get to them this evening." With those words, Mr. Oakley stepped over to Ruth's desk.

Ruth gave him a sweet, puzzled smile.

"You haven't even turned your computer on!" Mr. Oakley flicked on the switch. "You can't just sit here, you know. You're late joining this class as it is. I wish students wouldn't transfer in the middle of the year," he muttered. "It's difficult to get them up and running at the same pace as the rest of the class."

Ruth stared at the back of Mr. Oakley's head while he got the machine set up.

"I don't know how to work this particular machine," Ruth admitted.

"That's obvious," Mr. Oakley responded testily. He seemed to resent being saddled with a new student, especially when Ruth had difficulty understanding because of her hearing impairment.

Throughout the hour, Mr. Oakley's impatience

grew along with Ruth's bewilderment. Each time she struggled to make sense of something on the fading screen, the instructor gave her a brief, abrupt answer.

Lexi found herself gritting her teeth, feeling as though the hour would never end.

———

As the week stretched on, the atmosphere in Mr. Oakley's computer class grew more and more uncomfortable. Lexi had never been fond of Mr. Oakley, but now she was beginning to actively dislike him.

For some unexplained reason, he refused to recognize the fact that Ruth was having trouble because of her handicap. Instead, he acted as though it were because she was unwilling to follow his directions.

Lexi and Binky discussed the situation on their way home from school.

"Mr. Oakley is just plain mean," Binky said indignantly. "He's been horrid to Ruth. He assumes that if she doesn't understand something the first time through, she's not paying attention. All he'd have to do is look at her hearing aids to know that she has difficulty catching everything that's said."

Lexi couldn't agree more. "I've seen things like this happen before. There are people who can't deal with anyone who has a handicap or illness. They either ignore the handicap or they ignore the person. I know this because of our experiences with Ben."

"It's mean and inconsiderate," Binky concluded. "Ruth can't help being hearing-impaired any more than Ben can help being a child born with Down's syndrome. Mr. Oakley acts as if Ruth is the one at fault!"

———

As Lexi entered the computer classroom the next day, she tried to think what she could do to help Ruth. She hated to see her dismissed so rudely.

"We're going to do some more work with the function keys today," Mr. Oakley announced. "If you will open your manuals to page fifty-nine . . ."

Hesitantly, Ruth raised her hand.

"Oh no," Lexi muttered under her breath. Out of the corner of her eye, she could see Binky sinking lower in her chair.

"Now what?" Mr. Oakley was irate.

"What page was that, please?" Ruth asked.

Mr. Oakley glared at Ruth and repeated the number.

An expression of confusion crossed Ruth's face. "Ummm . . . I haven't finished the assignments in the previous chapter yet."

Lexi knew that Ruth was attempting to catch up by doing extra assignments. Fortunately, the work she did after school could be done on a better machine.

"If you can't keep up," Mr. Oakley said sharply, "perhaps you aren't ready to be in this class."

"I was in a computer class . . . at my other school," Ruth stammered. "This is a little . . . different. I just need a few days to catch up."

"It doesn't appear to me, Miss Miller, that you have much background on computer," Mr. Oakley pointed out coldly.

"But I was getting *A's*."

An expression of disbelief washed over Mr. Oakley's face. "Then what's your problem here?"

"If you could just turn my way when you speak . . ."

"Are you saying that *I'm* responsible for your inability to function in this class?" he asked indignantly.

Ruth flushed but held her ground. "Perhaps if I could look at the manual, I could work out things at home."

"I hardly view that as a satisfactory solution, Miss Miller. This is a lab class. You do your work in school—if you are able to do it at all. You don't seem capable of following along here."

"I think I could if you'd speak a little louder and not turn your back when you speak—"

Mr. Oakley was obviously provoked. He glared at Ruth as he spoke. "We're going to have to decide one of two things, young lady. Either you are capable of being in this class or you are not. The other students are doing just fine. It would be a severe disservice to hold back the entire class while you play *catch-up*."

"But—" Ruth tried to respond.

"Perhaps another school would be more suited to your needs, Miss Miller."

Mr. Oakley's meaning was obvious. He believed Ruth needed to enroll in a school for the deaf. He didn't think she should be mainstreamed with "normal" students.

Tension crackled in the air as the students shifted uneasily in their seats. The hostile atmosphere could be felt though no one spoke, and Ruth sat as still as stone, staring straight ahead.

Lexi thought about what Binky had said when Ruth first arrived. It was unfortunate they couldn't make a hearing aid that filtered out the negative, hurtful things people said.

Mercifully, the bell rang and everyone scrambled to escape the awkward situation. There was a traffic jam in the doorway as everyone pressed to get out. No one wanted to speak to Mr. Oakley, or to Ruth for that matter. It was just too painful to deal with.

"Come on, Lexi, let's get out of here," Binky whispered.

"No, Binky. I want to talk to Ruth." Lexi left the classroom but backed up against the wall outside the door. "Did you see the look on her face?" Lexi could feel her anger rise to the surface. "Mr. Oakley was cruel to her. He's treating her like a second-class citizen who doesn't have any feelings. I want to tell her that I think Mr. Oakley is wrong—"

Suddenly Ruth bolted past them and down the hall.

"Ruth, wait!" Lexi reached out to her but it was too late. She had already managed to disappear into the crowd.

"Did you see her face?" Binky's voice was barely above a whisper.

Lexi had caught a glimpse of Ruth's pale face and tear-filled eyes. She peeked into the computer room. Mr. Oakley sat calmly at his desk correcting papers.

Lexi's stomach lurched. For the rest of the morning she was not able to rid herself of the image of Ruth leaving the classroom or of Mr. Oakley working as if nothing had happened.

By noon Lexi's anger had not subsided. She set her lunch tray down abruptly and almost spilled her glass of milk.

Egg whistled through his teeth. "Weather report: storm clouds on the horizon. Hurricane Lexi is just off the east coast. Batten down the hatches; it looks like it's going to be a bad one."

Lexi was so rarely angry that she startled her friends.

"I am so furious I don't know what to do," Lexi said, sitting down hard on the bench. Peggy and Binky hung back, speechless.

"Binky told us what happened in computer class," Todd said.

"The more I think about Mr. Oakley's unfair treatment of Ruth, the more upset I become." Lexi ran her fingers through her hair. "I wish I'd said something to him at the end of class."

"You would have dared?" Binky gasped.

"Obviously, I didn't. But I think someone should have said something. It was so wrong of him."

Jennifer pushed aside her lunch tray. "Maybe. But don't blame yourself, Lexi. It doesn't always work to help everyone. You were a big help to me by challenging my attitude toward algebra. But I blew it again. I was sure I understood the lesson last night, but when I got to class I found out I'd done everything all wrong."

"I should have said something," Lexi repeated. "Mr. Oakley had no right to humiliate Ruth in class. He doesn't have any patience with anyone who doesn't catch on right away. It's just not fair."

"I worked half the night on this stuff," Jennifer said, following her own train of thought. "It was perfect. I was sure of it. Then when I got to class, I found out how wrong I was."

"Attitude. It's all a matter of attitude," Lexi continued. "Mr. Oakley has a terrible attitude."

"That's what I keep telling myself. If I keep up a

positive attitude, I'll get the hang of this algebra class," Jennifer said brightly.

"Do either of you realize what you're saying?" Todd interrupted. "There are two one-sided conversations going on here."

Lexi flushed slightly. "Sorry. I've been letting this build all day. I had to release a little steam."

"Me, too," Jennifer admitted. "I guess I shouldn't be worrying about my problem. It sounds as if the new girl is having some serious trouble."

"I don't know what to do about Ruth's problem," Todd said honestly. "But, I could try to answer some algebra questions for you, Jennifer, if you'd like me to."

"Wow! You'd do that for me?"

"It'd be better than listening to you complain about how hard algebra is for you," Todd teased. "I'm free last hour. Want to meet me in the library?"

"Sure! That'll be great." Jennifer looked sympathetically at Lexi. "Now all we have to do is figure out how Lexi can help Ruth Miller."

———

Lexi had difficulty concentrating in chemistry class. She stared at her textbook, but instead of seeing the words and figures, she pictured Ruth's sad face. She ached for the new girl, trying to imagine what it would be like to be in her position.

After that class, Lexi breezed into the music room to return some sheet music and almost collided with Mrs. Waverly.

"Whoa!" Mrs. Waverly peered over the top of a stack of sheet music. "What's your hurry, Lexi? You almost knocked these papers out of my hands."

"Sorry. I didn't see you. Are you all right?"

"Of course." Mrs. Waverly set the stack of music down on the table. "The question is, are *you* all right?"

"Ummmm. I don't know!" Lexi sank into a chair and put her head in her hands.

Mrs. Waverly lightly touched her shoulder. "Want to talk about it?"

"It's not really my business," Lexi began. "But it's just so *unfair*!"

"What's unfair?"

The whole scene between Ruth and Mr. Oakley in the computer class poured out.

Mrs. Waverly listened quietly until Lexi was finished. "That's quite an accusation, Lexi. Are you sure about it?"

"Positive. I was there. Mr. Oakley isn't giving Ruth a fair chance!"

Mrs. Waverly was silent a moment. "I'm glad you told me, Lexi. Maybe I can help."

Lexi looked up hopefully. "Could you?"

"I have a meeting with the principal next hour to discuss my music budget. I could mention the incident to him. Better yet, I could speak to Mr. Oakley. I have pretty good rapport with him."

"Do you think it would do any good?"

"I think so. Mr. Oakley is a young, inexperienced teacher. He probably has no idea how hurtful this behavior can be. Many people are uneducated about certain handicaps, and consequently are a little afraid of them. Perhaps Mr. Oakley needs to be encouraged to see Ruth as a student of equal importance and value, rather than a burden."

"I'd really appreciate your talking to him, Mrs. Waverly."

"I'll see what I can do. But if the situation doesn't get better, you and Ruth may have to go to the principal with your complaint."

"Thanks," Lexi said simply. She was relieved to know that Mrs. Waverly was willing to help, however doubtful she was of the impact anyone could have on Mr. Oakley.

After school, Lexi stopped Peggy in the hallway. "Are you walking home?"

"I'm going to the church, first, remember?"

"Oh, that's right."

Once a week Peggy attended a group meeting for teenagers with alcohol-related problems. Since Peggy had joined the group, Lexi had seen some noticeable changes in her friend.

"How's it going? The support group, I mean."

"Good. It grows a little each month. There are more and more teens finding out about the group and realizing they need help."

"How about yourself? How are you doing?"

"I just take it one step at a time, Lexi. I try not to look too far into the future or too deep into the past." Peggy glanced at her watch. "I'd better get going or I'll be late. Sorry I can't walk with you. Maybe Binky's still around."

"She has an appointment at the eye doctor this afternoon."

"Well, see you later."

Lexi nodded and turned to her locker. She gathered the books she needed and left the school alone.

Chapter Five

"Wait up, Ruth!" Lexi called as she hurried down the school steps. "I need to talk to you."

Ruth stopped immediately. "I looked around for you after school but couldn't find you."

"I was talking to Peggy. You must have just missed me." Lexi smiled. "I'm glad we found each other. I have something important to tell you."

Lexi felt a nervous quiver in her stomach. Would Ruth think her a busybody for interfering in her life?

"I talked to Mrs. Waverly today," Lexi blurted.

"The music teacher, right?"

"Right. We talked about you . . . and Mr. Oakley."

"Oh? Why?"

Lexi kicked at some loose stones on the sidewalk. "I've been upset about the way Mr. Oakley has been treating you. I told Mrs. Waverly about it."

Ruth's step slowed. "What did she say?"

"That she'd try to talk to Mr. Oakley. She said he's a young, inexperienced teacher, that he has a lot to learn about people with handicaps." Lexi looked anxiously at Ruth. "Do you mind? I hope you don't think I'm meddling in your business. It's just that Oakley is such a—"

"It's okay. I've been trying to build up the courage

47

to tell my aunt what's been happening in class. But I'm afraid if I do, she'll go to the administration and there could be a big uproar . . ."

"And Oakley might treat you worse than ever?"

"Something like that."

"If Mrs. Waverly can't handle it, no one can. She's great, Ruth. Really."

"Maybe it's a good thing you said something. Now maybe I won't have to." Ruth blushed slightly. "I'm such a coward."

"No you're not. Mr. Oakley is a bully. I don't think he could handle it very well if the shoe were on the other foot—if *he* were the one who couldn't understand."

Ruth's eyes lit up, and she began to move her hands in a graceful fashion.

"What are you doing?" Lexi asked.

"Signing the words: 'I'd like to show him a thing or two!' I wonder how he'd feel if everyone communicated like this except him!"

"A taste of his own medicine. I think that's just what Mr. Oakley needs!"

Ruth pointed toward an old house just ahead. "That's where my aunt lives."

"Really? You're only a few blocks from my house."

Ruth paused in front of the big two-story manse. "Would you like to come inside? You don't have to stay long if you're busy."

"I'd love to. Thanks for asking."

The house appeared to have been built at the turn of the century. As they entered the foyer, Lexi marveled at the ornately carved woodwork and stained glass windows. A beautiful oak staircase led to the second floor.

"My grandparents lived here," Ruth explained. "Aunt Frances hasn't changed anything since."

Lexi found it a little unusual. It was as if the house were frozen in time, while the surrounding homes had been renovated and updated.

The living room was bright. Lace curtains hung loosely at the windows, and a cheerful yellow mum plant graced the coffee table.

"Aunt Fran must be in the kitchen." Ruth led the way through a winding hallway to the back of the house, where a robust, rosy-cheeked woman stood over the counter kneading bread.

"Ruth! Home from school already?" She looked up from a floured board. "And you've brought company. How nice. Please excuse the mess. I thought a little homemade bread would be nice with our stew for supper."

"It smells wonderful in here," Lexi said. "I'm Lexi Leighton. We live just a few blocks away."

Aunt Fran nodded knowingly. "Dr. Leighton's daughter, I presume."

"Yes, how did you know?" Lexi was surprised.

"I have to keep on top of things," she said with a chuckle. "You never know when Wilberforce here might need a doctor." She gestured toward the small gray poodle that sat in a well-worn plaid chair near the table. The dog wore a pert bright blue hat over one ear and blue booties on his feet.

"I've heard good things about Dr. Leighton's practice," Aunt Fran continued. "When it's time for Willy's next check-up, I'm going to take him there."

She noticed that Lexi looked amused at the dog's booties. Fran chuckled lightly. "It was spitting rain a little while ago and Willy wanted to go outside. I put his boots on, so as not to track mud, you know. By then he'd changed his mind." She shrugged. "Poodles do have a mind of their own."

Aunt Fran wiped her floured hands on her white apron. "I baked gingerbread this afternoon too. Ruth, maybe you and your friend would like a piece. I have whipped cream and applesauce."

Lexi's mouth watered at the thought, and she and Ruth sat down at the large oak table. Fran poured glasses of milk and served the warm cake. "I can't tell you how happy I am, Lexi, that Ruth has met you. She needs a friend—don't you, Ruthie?"

Ruth looked embarrassed.

"Her parents are going to be gone for a long time."

"I thought you would go to live with them eventually, Ruth."

Fran and Ruth exchanged glances.

"It all depends on how well Ruth gets along here. If we can manage to keep her happy, I'd like to have her stay for the rest of the school year." Aunt Fran smiled sweetly at her niece.

Lexi could tell that Ruth's aunt was very protective of her. She was certainly not timid about expressing herself.

"Ruthie has spent many years in a residential school for the deaf," Aunt Fran explained. "Her hearing is somewhat improved with her hearing aids, though, and as long as people speak naturally and clearly and she can catch some lip movement, she doesn't have any trouble at all—do you, Ruthie?"

Ruth and Lexi exchanged looks. Both were thinking of the dreadful scenes in computer class. Lexi caught the caution in Ruth's eyes and knew that Ruth didn't want her Aunt Frances to know yet

about the incidents with Mr. Oakley. Lexi felt sure
Fran would want to know if her niece were having
trouble in school, but Ruth's look kept her from
speaking about it.

"More milk?" Aunt Fran jumped from the table
and went to the refrigerator. "How about another
piece of gingerbread?"

"I'll ruin my supper," Lexi said. "But it was delicious." Lexi turned to Ruth. "Where else have you
lived besides Boston?"

Ruth gestured with her hands. "Everywhere."
She looked to her aunt, who expanded on where
they'd lived.

"My brother and his wife have been all over the
world. Africa. South America. Ruth was a world
traveler by the time she was five. Once she started
attending the deaf school, she remained in the
States, of course." Aunt Fran cast a worried glance
at her niece. "I hope that Ruth won't have too much
trouble adapting here in Cedar River. Have there
been any other deaf students in your high school?"

"None that I know of . . ." Lexi said. "But I
haven't been here that long myself."

"Did you like school today, Ruth?" her aunt
asked.

"History was good."

That would be Mr. Raddis's class, Lexi thought.
He was a very compassionate man.

"English was okay, science and math," Ruth continued. "Tomorrow I'm going to try out for choir." She
turned to Lexi. "I've never been in a choir before."

"Mrs. Waverly is great. Just watching her direct
makes you want to sing."

Lexi noticed Ruth was careful not to mention

computer class or Mr. Oakley. She wondered why she was so hesitant to tell her aunt about the trouble she had in that class.

Lexi wished other students at Cedar River would get to know Ruth as she had. She was really a sweet girl. Lexi knew all too well how many people feared those with handicaps. She hoped and prayed that Ruth would not be rejected for something she couldn't help.

"More cake, dear?" Fran offered again. "Ruth and I can't eat the whole thing ourselves. Just another sliver?"

"Thank you. But I can't eat another bite. It was wonderful though." Lexi decided she liked Ruth's aunt very much.

When Ruth took the dog outside, Aunt Fran grabbed Lexi's hand. "I want to thank you, my dear, for befriending Ruth. I've been praying that she'd have an easy transition into school at Cedar River. . . . You might be an answer to that prayer."

"How much does Ruth really understand?" Lexi ventured.

"A good share of what is said. When it was first discovered that Ruth had a serious hearing impairment, the family thought they might have to learn to sign. It's quite difficult you know. It takes a lot of practice. I learned finger spelling myself. You use hand and finger shapes to indicate letters of the alphabet."

"What's the difference between that and signing?"

"Finger spelling is a manual alphabet. It can even be used for people who are blind. Sign language, on the other hand, is hand shapes and movements and sometimes even facial expressions that indicate entire words or concepts. It's much more complicated. Ruth is proficient in both.

"Ruth has more difficulty lipreading or speech reading," Frances continued. "It's not easy for her."

"I can understand how it would be hard." Lexi recalled the afternoon she and her friends had stared at the television set trying to make sense of the program by reading lips.

"There's a lot of guess-work involved in lipreading. Especially if you join the middle of a conversation, and you don't have the advantage of having the drift of the topic from the beginning. Deaf children are taught to lip-read normal speech. Someone who speaks too quickly or slowly can throw them off."

"Some people don't move their lips much when they speak," Lexi added.

"That's right. And many sounds are made in the throat, and can't be detected on the lips. Lip-readers gather about half their information from lipreading. They must rely on their instincts and experience to fill in the blanks."

"Wow. There's so much I never knew," Lexi admitted.

"Ruth has an advantage in lipreading that children who are born completely deaf don't have."

"Why is that?"

"Ruth has heard most of the sounds in our language. Someone who has never heard them will have difficulty imagining them."

"Do you think she counts heavily on lipreading?"

"Frankly, I'm not sure. Ruth manages to gather information from one source or another. I always try to be sure she can see my face when I speak to her.

And I don't mumble or run words together. People who speak fast are harder to hear and to read, of course. I think Ruth depends on lipreading to fill in what she misses, even though her hearing aids have made a tremendous difference for her."

"It's good to know. I don't want to pry by asking her too many questions," Lexi explained.

"Oh, Ruth doesn't mind. It's actually *easier* for her when people do ask questions. Some people seem to pretend there's nothing wrong with her. Ruth knows people can see her hearing aids. She'd rather answer questions than have people pretend her problem doesn't exist."

Lexi was glad Ruth's aunt had taken the time to explain this to her.

Ruth returned to the kitchen just as they finished.

"Ruth, I've just been explaining to Lexi about the difficulties of the hearing-impaired. I know you don't mind. Why don't you tell her about the new telephone we've ordered?"

"Our new telephone will have a light on it as well as a bell," Ruth explained with a faint smile. "That way, even if I don't hear the phone, I'll be able to see that someone is calling."

"We could order a doorbell with a flashing light also," Aunt Fran said. "But I'm not sure we need that. I don't leave the house that much without Ruth." Aunt Frances slapped her hand on her knee. "You should see Ruth's alarm clock!"

Lexi was amazed. It had never occurred to her that someone who was hearing-impaired may not hear an alarm clock. But of course they probably took their hearing aids off at night. "How does it work?"

"It's attached to a pad beneath her pillow. When the pad begins to vibrate, Ruth knows it's time to get up."

Lexi laughed. "Maybe that's what I need. My mother says it would take an earthquake to wake me some mornings."

Lexi gave a startled gasp as a big yellow cat suddenly jumped onto her lap, digging its claws into her legs.

"Sorry about that." Ruth scooped the cat into her arms. "He must have frightened you."

"He startled me anyway," Lexi admitted, rubbing her legs.

Ruth buried her face in the animal's soft fur, closing her eyes as she smiled happily.

"Tiger is Ruth's cat," Aunt Fran explained. "I think he's one of the reasons she agreed to stay with me instead of going with her parents. She would have had to leave him behind."

Ruth looked up at Lexi. "Well, I would miss having him jump up on my bed every morning. I can feel him purring."

"*Feel* him purr . . ." *Of course*, Lexi thought. Even if Ruth couldn't hear her cat in the morning, she'd be able to feel the rumbling of the big cat's body when it purred. A whole new world was opening up to Lexi—the world of the deaf and hearing-impaired. She was understanding more and more about Ruth.

Lexi glanced at the clock on the wall. "I'd better be going. Thanks again for the great snack."

"Thank *you* for coming in," Ruth's aunt said as she and Ruth walked Lexi to the front door.

"See you tomorrow, Ruth." Lexi smiled and Ruth nodded shyly. She stood on the steps and waved until Lexi turned the corner.

Lexi walked slowly, thinking about all she'd learned visiting with Ruth and her aunt. How lonely it must be to be separated from your parents and to be cut off from others too because of a hearing loss. Lexi was beginning to comprehend what real loneliness must be.

She thought of the time her class had studied about Helen Keller. She was quoted as saying that blindness separated people from things in the world, but deafness separated people from other people. Now Lexi realized what she meant.

Lexi prayed for Ruth as she walked. She also prayed for Mr. Oakley, that he would have compassion and understanding for Ruth, not just impatience. Lexi also prayed for herself, asking God for wisdom to help Ruth in her computer class, thanking Him for the gifts of sight and hearing that she'd taken for granted until now.

Chapter Six

Lexi was in her bedroom doing homework when she heard the doorbell ring, and then Ben's footsteps across the living room. She heard him open the door and give his cheery hello.

Next, Ben bounded up the stairs to Lexi's bedroom. The door was ajar and he burst in without knocking. Benjamin's beautiful brown eyes were wide with concern.

"It's for you, Lexi," he said breathlessly.

Lexi's stomach lurched. "What is it, Ben? Who's here?"

"It's Binky."

"Oh." Lexi's shoulders relaxed. "Why are you so upset?"

"Binky's crying, Lexi." Ben's compassionate nature could not tolerate tears. "She's standing at the front door crying."

Lexi pushed away from her desk and hurried past her little brother and down the stairs.

Binky was leaning against the door frame mopping her nose and eyes with a well-used tissue. When she saw Lexi she burst into tears.

"Bink, *what* is wrong?" Lexi slid her arm around her friend and led her into the living room, sitting her down on the couch. She perched next to Binky and looked into her eyes. "Will you please tell me what's happened?"

"It's terrible, Lexi. Just terrible. The most awful thing in the world has happened." Binky's chin quivered, then she began to sob openly.

Lexi reached for a box of tissue and stuffed a wad into Binky's hand. She'd never seen her so upset.

"Binky, *tell* me! How can I help if you won't tell me what's wrong?"

"You can't help me," Binky sobbed. "No one can."

"Binky, you're scaring me now."

"Don't be scared, Lexi. It's just that . . . I . . . I . . . have to get *glasses*." Binky flopped back against the couch weeping and howling in despair.

Lexi blinked twice. *Glasses?* "Glasses? That's *it*? You have to get glasses?"

"My mom took me . . . hmmm . . . to the eye doctor this afternoon," Binky stammered. "He said I needed glasses. No question about it."

Lexi's shoulders sagged in relief. "So that's all that's wrong? You just need to get glasses?"

Binky straightened up in a sudden huff. "What do you mean, is that *all* that's wrong? I think that's a *lot* to be wrong." Binky was indignant, her tears suddenly deferred. "Why *me,* Lexi? Do you realize how terrible I'm going to look?"

Binky jumped up and stared into the mirror over the fireplace. Her nose was red and her eyes puffy. "I'm going to look worse than ever, Lexi. I'm not pretty like you are. When I put those big ugly frames on my face, I'm going to look like a geek." Binky gawked anxiously into the mirror. "I'm plain and unattractive now. When I get glasses, there'll be absolutely no hope!"

Even though Lexi had to stifle an urge to giggle, she felt sympathy for her friend. Binky had always been self-conscious about her looks, about the fact that she appeared younger than her classmates.

"I can hear it already," Binky moaned. "I'll be 'old four-eyes' for the rest of my life."

"That was Teddy Roosevelt," Lexi reminded Binky, trying to hide her smile.

"I don't care who it was. Now it's going to be me!" Binky paced back and forth across the living room floor like a caged animal. "Why, Lexi? That's all I want to know. Why me? I'm already short, skinny, and have Egg for a brother. Isn't that enough strikes against a single human being?

"Of course I had to try on frames, but they all looked alike to me—ugly. The wire ones look too old. The plastic ones look too young. They all make me look like Miss Studious. I can just hear the teasing."

Lexi let Binky rant on. It seemed to help her calm down.

"The doctor says I don't need to wear them all the time, but that I do need glasses for school." She snapped her fingers. "Maybe I could wear them when I leave the house, put them in my locker, and bring them home again. Mom would think I wore them at school." Binky shot Lexi an appraising glance. "You wouldn't tell on me, would you?"

"Well, you *have* been squinting at the blackboard," Lexi reminded her.

"That's not my fault!" Binky was quick to point out. "It's because the teachers write so small. And the chalk is poor too. The writing is too light. Haven't you noticed?"

"No, I haven't, Binky."

"Well, it's true. It's the teachers' fault; that's all there is to it. Maybe I can ask them to write bigger and more clearly." She slapped her knee. "That's what I'll do! Teachers are paid to teach effectively. They aren't being very effective when they have cramped handwriting and use bad chalk!"

Binky was so busy convincing herself, she didn't realize how ridiculous she sounded. "I could sit at the front of the room instead of the back! Of course only a nerd would choose to sit at the front of the room," she mumbled. She chewed on her lower lip, considering that problem. "If I could get the teachers to make up new seating charts, everyone would have to move and I might end up in the front row."

Binky was still mentally rearranging classrooms when the doorbell rang again. Lexi got up to answer it.

"Hi, what's up?" Lexi greeted Peggy Madison, who looked fresh and bright in a new outfit of mint-green leggings and a long mint and peach-colored bulky top.

"Come in, Peggy. We're having a crisis here. Binky just arrived with some bad news."

"Bad news?"

"She has to get glasses," Lexi explained.

Peggy shrugged. "Glasses? What's the big deal?"

"She thinks it's a conspiracy to make her look ugly. Now she's blaming the teachers for writing too small and making her sit at the back of the room."

Peggy grasped the situation immediately. When they entered the living room she smiled at Binky. "Hi, Bink. I hear you're going to get glasses. That's great!"

"Great? You must be crazy!" Binky's lower lip began to quiver again. "It's terrible. It's awful. It's horrible. They're . . . disfiguring!"

"No, Binky. Glasses aren't so bad. Lots of people wear them," Peggy tried to console her.

"Right. Like my grandmother."

"Binky McNaughton," Peggy said sternly. "There are zillions of things worse than wearing glasses."

"Not for me there aren't. I'm not pretty. Glasses are going to make me look . . . goofy!"

Peggy rolled her eyes. "The last time my mom and I were at the mall, we went into an optical shop just to look around. We tried on frames just for the fun of it."

"You tried on frames for the fun of it?"

"Sure. We decided some of the frames were so flattering we'd like to wear glasses even though we don't need them."

"You are sick, Peggy Madison," Binky said grumpily. "Sick, sick, sick."

"I tend to agree with Peggy," Lexi interjected. "Some frames look so good, the person looks better *with* glasses than without them."

"Yeah, right. You're just trying to con me into thinking glasses are okay," Binky moped.

"Look at Minda," Peggy quipped. "Haven't you seen her in her fashion frames?"

Binky scowled. "That's different. Those frames have clear glass for lenses. She wears them as fashion accessories. When she wears her turquoise sweater she wears the turquoise frames. Big deal; she doesn't *have* to wear them!"

"But who in the entire school is more fashion conscious than Minda Hannaford? If *she* thinks glasses can be a fashion accessory, why couldn't yours be?" Peggy argued.

Binky was thoughtful. "I guess my cousin looks kind of nice in glasses . . . Of course, she's a lot prettier than I am."

"Binky, you're adorable," Lexi said, smiling.

"Adorable?" Binky shot back. "What kind of a compliment is that? It sounds like you're talking to a five-year-old."

Lexi was quick to remedy her comment. "That's the other good thing about glasses. Sometimes they make people look a little older, more mature."

"Older?" Binky savored the word like a treasure. "Do you really think so?"

"Sure. With glasses you'd probably look . . . eighteen!"

"Eighteen?"

"Or even nineteen."

"Hmmmm." Binky sat back, musing over this new twist. "Do you really think glasses could make me look . . . college age?"

"Definitely," Lexi assured her. "And the preppy look is really in now."

"Like I said," Peggy affirmed, "there are worse things in life than having to wear glasses. Think about Ruth Miller. How would you like to have to wear hearing aids? Ruth's never going to be able to hide her deafness. You, on the other hand, may be able to get contact lenses someday."

Binky stared at her friends. Suddenly her face crumpled and she dissolved in tears once again. "Oh, Peggy, Lexi, how could I have been so selfish? I feel so guilty. How could I have thought wearing glasses was such a serious problem?"

Binky sank dejectedly into the couch cushions. "Now, I *really* feel guilty."

"No one wants you to feel guilty, Binky," Lexi soothed. "We just want you to put your problem into perspective. Having to wear glasses may not be your idea of fun, but Peggy is right. Your news could have been a lot worse."

"I feel awful. I've been selfish and foolish." Binky's mouth turned downward in a pout. "Poor Ruth. How can she stand it? Not being able to hear and having to wear those awful hearing aids . . ."

"Ruth's going to have a hard time in school," Peggy said matter-of-factly as she sat across from Lexi and Binky.

"Why's that?" Lexi asked.

"I heard the Hi-Fives talking about her today." Peggy looked down, shaking her head. "They were being really cruel."

"I'm not surprised," Binky added.

"You know how they are. They dissect people like bugs in biology. They said Ruth was plain, dull, and that her clothes were ugly."

"How thoughtless!" Lexi said.

"Immature is more accurate," Binky added.

"How about just plain dumb?" Peggy stated flatly. "I keep hoping they'll grow up, but it hasn't happened yet."

"Sometimes people go through their whole lives being insensitive to others," Lexi commented seriously. "It's as if they have blinders on and can't see the hurt they're causing. If something is true or funny, they take it as license to say it at the expense of another's reputation or feelings."

"It's not just the Hi-Fives," Peggy continued.

"Lots of kids are making fun of Ruth. I heard some-one call her a 'retard,' but I don't think she heard them."

"People can be so awful!" Binky was indignant.

"When they don't understand a handicap they shun the person," Lexi explained. "I know from ex-perience with Ben. Some people are afraid of hand-icaps. Maybe they fear the disability will rub off on them somehow. They don't seem to realize that han-dicapped people have emotions, feelings, dreams, and hopes too, just like everyone else."

"Just because Ruth can't *hear* the hurtful com-ments, doesn't mean she can't be hurt by them," Binky summed up.

"That's right," Peggy agreed. "Ruth can *see* peo-ple avoiding her, laughing at her, or pointing a finger. She can see that people aren't as friendly to her as they are to others."

"I guess having to wear glasses isn't so bad after all," Binky murmured.

"I wonder how Ruth can handle it," Peggy won-dered aloud. "It must be tough. I know how badly I've handled some things that have happened to me."

"I think Ruth has a lot of patience," Lexi com-mented. "If she waits long enough, maybe some of these people will come to their senses and become her friends."

Binky rocked back and forth moaning softly. "Oh, I feel so guilty."

"Binky, don't feel guilty. You can befriend Ruth tomorrow. She'll need all the friends she can get."

The thought seemed to satisfy Binky. "I wonder what made her deaf. Do you suppose it was a birth defect? Or some disease?"

As the girls speculated for a moment on what may have caused Ruth's condition, Ben meandered into the living room, walked over to Binky and caressed her face in his small hands.

"Are you better now?" he asked sweetly. "Don't cry anymore, okay? It makes Ben sad."

Binky sighed, and scooped Ben into her arms for a bear hug. Ben squirmed and giggled.

"You're such a sweetheart, Benjamin Leighton," she murmured into his silky black hair.

"I'm a sweetheart." Ben crawled out of her grasp. "Binky's going to look pretty in glasses!" he announced, betraying the fact that he'd been eavesdropping.

Binky kissed Ben's forehead. "Pretty? Is that what you think? Really?"

"*Very* pretty."

"I'm glad you said that, Ben. I'm going to have my new glasses just in time for the church retreat!"

Chapter Seven

"Hey, Ruth! Your shoes are untied. Be careful, you might trip," a ninth-grade boy called to her.

"Her shoes aren't untied," Lexi said between clenched teeth.

"We can tell her anything we want. She can't hear us anyway," another boy said.

"I can't believe you guys. Leave her alone, do you hear me?" Lexi grabbed one of them by the collar.

"Hey! Let go!" The boy shrugged out of Lexi's grasp. "Besides, she doesn't care. She can't hear anything."

"Calm down, Lexi." Jennifer put a hand on Lexi's arm. "They're just being dumb."

"They're being mean," Lexi retorted.

"Immature. If Ruth can ignore them, you can too."

"Is Ruth ignoring them? Or is it that she can't hear what's going on?"

"I don't know. The hearing aids seem to help. She's probably learned the best way to cope with the teasing is to ignore it."

Lexi was still upset when she entered music class. A flood of students pushed to find their places before Mrs. Waverly tapped her baton on the music stand.

"Sit down, people. There is no need to push. There is plenty of time and plenty of space," Mrs. Waverly spoke to the unruly students.

The two boys who'd been taunting Ruth entered the room. "Hey! Look who's here! It's that deaf girl."

"What are you doing here?" The boy spoke loudly and looked right at Ruth. "A deaf person in a music class?"

Mrs. Waverly, who had turned to write on the blackboard, spun around. "What did you say, young man?"

The boy scooted backward to his chair and landed in the seat with a thump. "Nothing, I . . ."

"*My* hearing is just fine, thank you," Mrs. Waverly said with deadly calm. "Please repeat what you just said."

"I . . . I asked her how come she was in music class, being deaf and all," he stammered. "Deaf people can't sing or play instruments, can they?" he continued, growing braver as the giggles grew louder. "What's the point of being in a music class if you can't hear the music?"

More titters erupted from the back of the room.

Mrs. Waverly cast a warning glance over the group. Her expression softened when she looked at Ruth. "Ruth, did you hear everything the boy said?"

Ruth sat stoically, silent as a statue. Then she nodded slowly.

Mrs. Waverly glared at the outspoken boy. "You will apologize to Ruth right now."

"I . . . uh . . ."

"*Now!*" Mrs. Waverly's voice rose dramatically.

"I'm sorry. I . . . I didn't know you could hear me." The boy dropped his gaze to the floor.

"I am very disappointed with this kind of behavior," Mrs. Waverly continued. "Some of you have shown an appalling lack of compassion and maturity. *All* people, regardless of their abilities or disabilities, should be treated with respect and kindness."

Every eye in the room was riveted on Mrs. Waverly. She was without doubt one of Cedar River High's most respected teachers. Even though the incident had obviously angered her, there would be no tirade. Instead, they got a lecture on a famous composer.

"I'd like to talk to you today about one of the finest composers of our time: Ludwig van Beethoven."

There was some shuffling of feet and a few sighs from the back row.

Mrs. Waverly continued. "Beethoven was born in 1770, and died in 1827. Though he didn't live a long life by today's standards, he lived a full one."

"He's my mom's favorite composer," Tim Anders blurted out.

"That's great, Tim. Can anyone else tell us something more about Beethoven?"

The room was filled with tense silence.

"There is no other outstanding feature about Beethoven that someone would like to point out?"

Silence.

Mrs. Waverly's attention focused on Ruth in the front row. A smile began to spread over Ruth's face. "Is there anything you can tell the class about Beethoven, Ruth?"

"He was deaf." Ruth's voice was soft, her words evenly spoken, but they could be heard in the back row.

"Deaf?" An incredulous ninth-grader spoke up.

"How can a composer be deaf? That doesn't make any sense."

"Well, it's true," Mrs. Waverly affirmed. "And even though it was the most devastating thing that could happen to a man of such musical genius, Beethoven was still able to compose many marvelous musical scores in spite of his handicap."

"But how? How could he do that?" Gina Williams wondered aloud.

"Beethoven was accomplished at the piano, the violin, and the viola. He had been for many years. When he lost his hearing, he carried the memory of the sound and musical notes in his mind. Though he could no longer play the instruments, he still heard them in his mind and was able to write music."

"He had to quit playing the piano?" someone asked.

"Yes. A great tragedy, don't you think? It must have been humiliating for a man of such wonderful musical talent to no longer be able to translate it to the piano. As his sense of hearing deteriorated, he began communicating by writing notes on paper. His frustration showed itself in many ways."

"How awful," Egg mused aloud, "to have done something so well, and then to have to give it up, to feel yourself losing the ability you once had."

The class remained very quiet and attentive. Lexi had never known the class to be so still. Every eye was on Mrs. Waverly. Occasionally someone looked at Ruth, who remained poised at her desk.

"Beethoven is not the only famous person who was deaf," Mrs. Waverly went on. "Francisco Goya, the Spanish artist, also became deaf later in life. He was more fortunate than Beethoven, of course, in that his particular talent did not require that he have his sense of hearing intact. Though he was deaf for nearly thirty-five years, the calamity never prevented him from creating his famous paintings."

More students were casting curious glances at Ruth, perhaps seeing her in a new light.

"Most of you have read *Gulliver's Travels* in your English literature class," Mrs. Waverly said. "The author, Jonathon Swift, suffered a hearing loss also, though he did not allow it to affect his creations of brilliant literary satire.

"Being deaf as an artist or writer would not be as serious a handicap as it would be for a deaf musician, of course, but think what it would be like to be deaf if you were an inventor. Thomas Edison, a great inventor from our own country, was also hearing-impaired. Yet his disability did not keep him from inventing the electric light, the telegraph, and what was considered the most innovative instrument of its time: the phonograph. Edison invented a machine that reproduced sound waves—even though he had to struggle to hear them himself."

"Could deafness ever be considered an advantage?" Egg ventured.

"Perhaps. In some ways Edison's hearing handicap forced him into a life that held little distraction. And he didn't have all the interruptions we may have in a day. Instead, he had the benefit of total concentration. Perhaps being freed from superfluous noise allowed him to become the fine inventor that he was."

"So maybe it was *good* for Edison to be hearing-impaired?" Tim Anders asked.

"That's only a theory," Mrs. Waverly answered, "but possibly true. Deaf people, because of the nature of their handicap, are forced to turn inward, to become more speculative, to rely more on themselves. Much of the time, of course, they are cut off from the rest of the world that hears and speaks clearly."

The ninth-grade boy who had teased Ruth before the class began to squirm in his seat. "I never knew any of this stuff before," he blurted.

Ruth smiled slightly.

Mrs. Waverly studied the class quietly for a moment. "We are very fortunate to have Ruth in our class. Just like the famous people I have mentioned, Ruth is proof to us that being hearing-impaired does not mean that she lacks talent or intelligence. I don't want to embarrass Ruth, but people with handicaps have feelings just like the rest of us. Let's make certain the behavior we witnessed today is never repeated. Each of you in this class can help others in the school to become educated along these lines. I hope I can count on the cooperation of all of you."

Mrs. Waverly directed her attention to the front row. "Ruth, I'm sorry you've had to experience what you have in your first weeks at Cedar River. I'd like to apologize on behalf of our student body and faculty. Maybe we can begin again on a fresh note. Would you like to play for everyone the piece you played earlier for me?"

There were gasps and whispers throughout the room. It seemed no one had known that Ruth could play the piano.

Smiling shyly, Ruth rose slowly from her desk and walked to the grand piano. Without fanfare, she sat down at the bench and gently brushed her fingers over the keys without depressing them. Then she closed her eyes for a moment, recalling the music in her mind. Effortlessly, she began to play a Mozart sonata.

Lexi recognized the music from an appreciation seminar Mrs. Waverly had given last spring. Ruth's music was not only recognizable, it was very *good*.

As she struck the last chords, Ruth looked up to the concentrated gaze of the entire class. Egg rose first, clapping vigorously, and soon others followed until the whole class was giving Ruth a standing ovation.

Taking advantage of her captivated audience, Ruth stood and spoke: "I have a friend who goes to a church for deaf people. They have amplifiers installed under the seats so that the people can feel the music vibrating beneath them. Actually, with these hearing aids I can hear more than you might think. They enable me to attend a conventional school. I appreciate your patience in helping me to adjust here."

Mrs. Waverly made no attempt to resume control of the class. The questions concerning Ruth's musical ability and her deafness kept coming until the class bell rang. The room had nearly emptied when Ruth picked up her books.

Minda held back and walked her out the door. "Good job," she said, barely above a whisper.

Ruth had no trouble reading her lips. She gave Minda a bright smile. "Thank you."

Minda proceeded down the hall alone, her usual superior attitude gone for the moment.

"Did you see that?" Jennifer whispered.

"Minda being nice to Ruth?" Binky asked. "Pinch me quick. I think I'm dreaming."

Lexi pinched them both before hurrying off to her next class.

———

"She was great, wasn't she?" Lexi heard someone say after school. "I couldn't believe she could play the piano."

"I didn't think people with a hearing loss could do things like that," someone else admitted.

"Mrs. Waverly was terrific. She sure showed those ninth-grade boys a thing or two." The halls were buzzing with talk of Ruth's piano-playing skills and Mrs. Waverly's lecture on deafness. There was even some compassionate speculation about what it must be like to be deaf.

"Poor Ruth," Lexi murmured. "She's the topic of conversation no matter what."

"Well, at least now people know they're dealing with someone who's not a mindless airhead with no feelings," Binky stated flatly.

"Speaking of Ruth, where is she?"

"I saw her walking down the hall with her books under her arm a minute ago," Binky said. "She was probably in a hurry to get out of here today."

"Was she alone?" Lexi asked.

"I think so."

"Terrific. Everyone feels comfortable talking *about* her, but no one feels comfortable talking *to* her. Come on. Maybe we can still catch up with her."

Lexi, Peggy, and Binky hurried out of the school. They could see Ruth walking slowly from the parking lot.

"There she is."

"Slow down!" Peggy huffed as they ran toward Ruth. "I don't like running on days I don't practice basketball."

"At least you're in good shape," Binky said, trying to keep up with the two taller girls.

"Ruth! Wait!" Lexi called loudly.

Slowly, Ruth turned and she saw the three girls coming toward her. A bright smile spread over her pretty face.

"There's no point walking home alone when we're all going in the same direction," Lexi said when they caught up to her. "You don't mind do you?"

"Of course not."

"Why don't all of you come over to my house," Peggy suggested. "Mom usually bakes on Thursdays. There should be something good for snack."

Lexi and Binky nodded, and the three of them looked expectantly at Ruth.

"I can call my aunt and tell her where I am."

———

"How does it feel to be a celebrity?" Binky asked as she polished off the last of a powdered donut.

"Embarrassing," Ruth admitted. "I'm really not very good at the piano—just mediocre, but now people tell me how wonderful I was. I guess it was something Mrs. Waverly did to give me some recognition and self-esteem."

"I think it was neat," Peggy said. "Besides, who says you're not good at the piano? You're great compared to me!"

"I guess people were impressed that I could do anything at all."

"We've never had a person like you in our school before," Binky explained. "It's going to be hard on you being the first. You'll just have to teach us everything we need to know."

"I'm not much of a teacher, I'm afraid. Actually, I'm basically a very quiet person. I like to read." Ruth laughed lightly. "No problem there. I can hear just fine when I'm reading."

"Do you ever get lonely?" Binky persisted. "Reading's all right, but I like to have friends around me, too."

"I haven't had much chance to make many friends because I've always traveled so much with my family. Before I went to a residential school for the deaf here in the States, I moved around with my mom and dad. They've always believed in learning as much as they could about the culture and resources of the countries we've lived in. When we were in Africa, for instance, I would get up early in the morning to watch the sunrise. Occasionally, I'd even see elephants on the horizon."

"Wow! You are so lucky!"

"Yes, but not lucky enough to have many friends in the places I've lived. Not like here, anyway. Not like all of you."

"Well, we want to be your friends," Binky assured her.

"How do you get along so well?" Peggy asked Ruth. "I'm not sure I could if I were you."

"I've always had a hearing loss. I don't know what it's like to be any different." Ruth tapped a hearing aid. "These things really help. I'm fortunate that they do. For some people, a hearing aid would not do any good."

An anxious sound escaped Binky's lips. "I feel awful," she said in her usual dramatic manner. "I've been really upset because I have to get glasses. Every time I look at you, Ruth, I think about how difficult your life has been. I don't know what I'd do if something like that happened to me! You have to be a special person to manage like you do."

"No, I'm not special at all. In fact, I'm really very ordinary. The only thing different about me is that I don't believe what people tell me."

"What do you mean by that?" Lexi asked.

"Well, if someone tells me that I *can't* do something, I don't take their word for it. I used to believe others when they told me that because I was hearing-impaired I wouldn't be able to sing or play the piano or do well in school. Then I tried to prove them wrong. Now I realize I don't have to prove anything anymore."

"How did you come to that conclusion?" Lexi asked.

"We have a family friend who's hearing-impaired. He's a college professor. Every day he lectures students with normal hearing. He has to make himself understood, and not allow his handicap to limit what he teaches his students."

"That must be hard," Binky interjected.

"He says the one thing he's learned is that he can't depend on others to help him. Not everyone is interested in helping, for one thing, and people aren't always around to help. He's always told me that I have to work very hard to get what I want in life."

"There are people who will help you," Lexi encouraged. "Like all of us."

"I appreciate that, Lexi. But you can't be around me every minute of the day. I have to rely on my own resources. I've come to realize that if I don't hear something in class, instead of fretting about it, I either need to ask for extra help or study the book twice as hard. I used to tape lectures and ask my parents to help me understand the material at home. It's not always fun, but it works. My grades are good. I study a lot. I don't enjoy watching TV, and it's hard for me to talk on the telephone, so there's not much else to do but study. I'd like to be a doctor someday."

"A doctor? Ooooh, won't that be hard?" Binky asked, her eyes as big as saucers.

"It won't be easy, but neither is being deaf. I've managed so far."

Now that she was relaxed with friends, Ruth smiled more easily and her sense of humor came through. Lexi decided then and there that Ruth's personality and intelligence more than made up for her disability. She hoped everyone at school would soon begin to see Ruth for the fun person that she was instead of just "the deaf girl."

"My worst problem is my shyness," Ruth admitted. "It holds me back. I'd be shy even if I *weren't* hearing-impaired, but sometimes when people stare at me or I can't pick up the threads of a conversation, I just back into a shell." Ruth's expression turned comical. "I guess that's why some of my friends used to call me *turtle!*"

The girls all laughed. "You shouldn't have told us that," Peggy said mischievously. "The nickname might catch on."

"*Turtle*—what a rude name!" Binky giggled. "Well, I guess it's no worse than *Binky!*"

"Isn't it hard not to feel sorry for yourself?" Peggy asked, turning the conversation serious again.

"Not any more. At the school for the deaf we weren't allowed to feel sorry for ourselves. I tried to complain about how tough it was to have this disability, but I couldn't get anyone to pay any attention to me. All the instructors told me I'd just have to work a little harder to compensate for the abilities I didn't have. Lots of people with more severe problems than mine made it through. They coped with some real adversity." Ruth paused for a moment. "People who felt sorry for themselves didn't get along very well at the school. The goal there was to teach us how to succeed, not to settle for failure."

"Maybe we should have a class like that at Cedar River," Peggy suggested.

"It takes more work and effort for me to get an *A* in a class than it does a student who has no trouble hearing. I struggle sometimes to catch every word while others don't even listen." Ruth shook her head. "Some don't appreciate how lucky they are to have all their faculties."

The girls were quiet, thinking about what Ruth was saying.

"No one is perfect," Ruth went on. "We all have to do the best we can with what we've got."

Lexi thought of Jennifer's learning disability. It hadn't been easy for her, either.

A bright smile spread across Ruth's face. "I've been given a lot. I have wonderful parents who love me and who have taught me about Jesus Christ. I'm really luckier than lots of people who have their hearing but don't know Christ as their Savior."

Binky brightened. "Oh, you're a Christian, too, Ruth?"

"Yes. I probably wouldn't be doing so well if I weren't."

Lexi was impressed with Ruth's maturity, her common sense, and her boldness. She expressed herself beautifully in spite of the monotone quality of her voice. Lexi was sure her own life, and the lives of her friends, would be richer for having known Ruth.

"Hey, I've got an idea!" Binky exclaimed suddenly.

"What's that?" Ruth asked.

"You could teach us sign language!"

Ruth's eyes twinkled with interest. "Are you sure you want to learn?"

"I think it'd be great!" Peggy enthused.

"A lot of kids ask to learn," Ruth said. "But then after a while they get bored with it. After all, it's easier to talk with your mouth than with your hands."

"You probably had to work hard to learn our language; the least we can do is learn a little of yours," Binky reasoned.

"Good point!" Ruth said, laughing. She lifted her hands gracefully and made some quick motions. "Do you know what I said?"

They all stared at her blankly.

"That was *I love you.*"

"Oh, teach us!" Binky begged.

Soon the girls were working their fingers and hands, making signs and laughing at their awkwardness.

"You're so graceful, Ruth, and we're so clumsy," Peggy moaned, trying to position her hand correctly for a word.

"All it takes is practice."

Mrs. Madison walked into the living room. "Hello, girls. Need anything more to eat?"

Binky clutched her stomach and groaned. "If I eat

another bite, I'll explode. Besides, I'd better save myself for the church retreat on Saturday. Pastor Lake says we'll have more food than we know what to do with."

"Are all of you going?" Mrs. Madison asked.

They started to nod, then Lexi realized Ruth wouldn't know about the retreat. "Our church youth group is having a retreat this weekend. Would you like to go with us? It'll be a lot of fun."

"Yes, Ruth. We'd love to have you," Binky agreed.

Ruth hesitated. "But I don't know anyone . . ."

"That's exactly why you should go. You can meet some new people. And you'll like Pastor Lake. He's terrific," Peggy added.

"I'm not sure," Ruth said slowly. "Large groups are hard for me. It's hard to hear individuals when a lot of people are talking at once."

"We'll take turns!" Binky offered.

"Please think about it at least," Peggy urged.

A twinge of concern came over Lexi. Were they pushing their new friend too hard, too soon?

Chapter Eight

Lexi had arrived at school early to finish writing captions for the latest edition of the *Cedar River Review*. She wrapped up the last of her ideas, dropped them in an envelope and laid them on the editor's desk. As she left the *Review* workroom, Lexi heard Jennifer calling from the other end of the hall.

"Hey, Leighton, wait up. I need to talk to you." Jennifer jogged toward Lexi. "I'm glad I caught you. Have you seen Binky this morning?"

"I haven't seen anyone. I've been all locked up in there," Lexi said, tilting her head toward the school paper workroom. "Why? what's wrong with Binky?"

"She's acting really weird, for one thing. Downright *spooky*, in fact."

"So? When did that become a cause for worry?" Lexi joked. "A lot of the things she does are weird or spooky."

"I know, but this is different. I saw her as soon as I got to school, but she wouldn't talk to me. She was at the far end of the hall. When she saw me near the door of a classroom, she dodged inside as though she were hiding something."

"Maybe she didn't really see you after all."

"Then why did she come out, look over her shoulder at me, and jog down the hall and into another classroom? She acted as if she were being chased . . . but no one was behind her."

Lexi had no explanation.

"Then, to make matters worse, I saw her near the administration offices. When she saw me coming, she ducked behind a waste can and bent over like she was looking for something. The next time I saw her, she hid behind the open door of her locker and stuffed something into her pocket."

"Maybe she's playing hide-and-seek with herself."

"Very funny. It would make more sense if Egg were somewhere nearby tormenting her, but he was nowhere to be seen. I think Binky's hiding from me."

"Did you two have an argument?"

"No. We were getting along fine yesterday."

"Don't worry about it," Lexi consoled her friend. "Egg and Binky tend to do . . . unique . . . things all the time."

"I suppose so," Jennifer said. "But she's really being strange this time."

A few moments later, Lexi had the opportunity to experience firsthand what Jennifer was complaining about. As Lexi neared her locker, she saw that Binky had already arrived at hers. The door was open and Binky's head and shoulders were buried deep within her locker. Scraps of paper and pencil stubs were falling to the floor at Binky's feet.

"Good morning," Lexi said. She tapped Binky on the shoulder, but Binky did not turn around.

"Good morning," came the muffled reply.

"What are you looking for?" Lexi peered over Binky's shoulder.

"Stuff."

"What kind of *stuff*?"

"School stuff."

"Can I help you?"

"No," came the discouraged reply. "Nobody can help me."

"Binky. I can hardly hear you. Why don't you turn around and tell me what's wrong?"

"No!"

"Are you going to spend the entire day with your head in your locker?"

"Maybe."

Then, slowly, agonizingly, Binky withdrew from the locker and turned to face Lexi. She was wearing a brand new pair of glasses.

The frames were a perfect combination of wire and tortoise shell—surprisingly flattering to Binky's delicate features.

"Your new glasses!"

Suddenly all the clues to the puzzle of Binky's behavior fell into place.

"I hate them!" Binky's eyes narrowed behind the lenses. "I hate them. I hate them. I hate them."

"You look wonderful."

"I do not."

"You do too."

"Do not."

"Binky, they're beautiful. They make you look so . . ."

" . . . nerdy?"

"No. Intelligent. Scholarly. Mature."

"Mature? As in *older*?"

"Yes, really. You could pass for a senior."

"Me? A senior?" Binky's tone of voice was doubtful, but she touched the bow of her glasses with new respect.

"Hey, Bink, great specs!" Tim Anders sauntered by.

"Really?" Binky looked amazed. "Thank you."

A group of guys passed by, and Brian James paused for a moment to stare at Binky. "Not bad, McNaughton. Not bad at all." Then he caught up with his friends and disappeared down the hallway.

"Is *this* what you've been so busy trying to hide all morning?" Lexi demanded.

"Jennifer told you, huh?"

"She thought she'd done something to make you mad at her."

"I didn't want her to see what I looked like in these things."

"You look nice. There's nothing wrong with those glasses."

"Hey, Binky, I love your glasses," Anna Marie said, coming up behind them. "They look really great on you."

By the time the threesome had finished their conversation, Binky was visibly swelling with pride.

"People really like these, don't they?"

"Obviously. They like them a lot. What were you so worried about?" Lexi asked.

"Hi there, Four Eyes."

"That. I was worried about *that*." Binky pointed over Lexi's shoulder.

Lexi and Anna Marie turned around to see Egg grinning at his sister. "How's school going today, Four Eyes?"

"He's been harassing me all morning," Binky moaned.

"Just ignore Egg," Lexi advised. "He'll get over it by the end of the day. Then no one will say another thing about your glasses."

"I don't know about that, Lexi," Egg argued. "I'll remember Binky's glasses for a long time. After all, Four Eyes will probably have to wear them forever."

"Egg McNaughton, why don't you get a life?" Binky sputtered. "You're pitiful. If you had a brain you'd be dangerous."

Egg's eyes grew round and a little startled. "My, my, Four Eyes certainly has a temper, doesn't she?"

"Like I said, Egg, *get a life*."

Egg grinned broadly. "Whatever." He ambled off down the hall.

"*Now* do you understand why I was worried?"

"Egg's your brother, Binky. What did you expect?"

"I guess you're right." Binky rapidly dismissed her cause for concern. "But I feel so self-conscious. These things feel huge sitting on my nose. It's as if they're screaming, 'Look at me!' "

"I feel that way sometimes when I have a new haircut, Binky," Anna Marie added sympathetically. "You'll get used to them in a few days."

"Hey, McNaughton, nice specs." That was Minda. Lexi, Anna Marie, and Binky all spun around in amazement.

Minda was dressed in a green and white rugby shirt and white denim jeans. She wore a pair of fashion glasses in the same green as the stripe in her shirt. "They're cute," Minda continued. "If I had to wear glasses full time, I'd probably pick a pair just like yours."

Binky's jaw dropped so low Lexi wondered if it

might not stay that way. "You'd pick glasses like *these*?" Binky echoed.

"Sure, why not?" Minda touched the frame of her own glasses. "But since I don't need them, I think it's fun to wear all the fashion colors. I got three more pair at the mall on Saturday. Wait till you see the ones I'm going to wear tomorrow!" Minda smiled coyly and sauntered off.

Binky turned to Lexi and Anna Marie. "Did you hear that? *Minda* actually paid me a compliment."

"A *big* compliment," Anna Marie corrected.

"I picked out something that Minda Hannaford would have chosen?" Binky marveled. "Well, what do you know about that? If Minda and I have the same taste," Binky said proudly, "maybe I don't look so bad after all."

"Binky, we said you look *great!*" Lexi's words came with the shrill sound of the first bell. "But we're going to be late if we don't get going," she yelled above the din.

"All right," Binky said, falling into step with her friends. "I wonder if anyone will notice that I'm wearing glasses?"

———

Lexi met Ruth outside the door to the computer classroom. Mr. Oakley had not yet arrived. Every time they met each other, Lexi tried out her newly learned sign language.

"How are you?" Lexi asked with her hands.

"Wonderful!" Ruth answered.

Lexi didn't have many words in her "vocabulary" yet, but she liked to practice the ones she knew.

"I love you," she spelled with her hands.

Ruth giggled and answered, "I love you, too."

"What's going on here?" Mr. Oakley had come up behind them. He looked from Lexi to Ruth.

"We . . . we were just talking," Lexi stammered.

"Talking?"

"With our hands."

"And what were you saying?"

Lexi looked knowingly at Ruth. "I said . . ." and Lexi repeated her hand motions.

"And *I* said . . ." Ruth moved her hands swiftly and gracefully.

"How do you expect me to understand that?" Mr. Oakley asked. "I don't know sign language."

"It's kind of hard, isn't it?" Ruth said softly. "Just like it's hard for me to understand you when your back is to the classroom."

An array of emotions played on Mr. Oakley's face. First irritation and impatience, then comprehension, and finally, remorse. "I never thought about it quite that way before. I . . . uh, I guess you're right. If I make it a point to turn toward the class when I speak, will you interpret for me what you and Lexi were saying?"

"Sure. Lexi said, 'I love you.' And I said, 'I love you, too.' "

Mr. Oakley blushed faintly. "Oh. I guess I owe you girls an apology. I thought maybe you were talking about me." Mr. Oakley looked directly at Ruth. "According to Mrs. Waverly, I have a great deal to learn about the hearing-impaired. You'll have to be patient with me. Maybe you can be *my* teacher."

Ruth simply smiled from ear to ear.

Chapter Nine

Lexi lay across her bed, her head propped with pillows, and the telephone resting on her middle as she talked with Todd.

"Did you ask the doctor about the retreat?" Lexi's voice was hopeful.

"Yeah. He says I can't go. It's too early. I told him that I wouldn't be doing anything strenuous or dangerous, but he still recommended I stay home. He thinks school is enough for me right now. He doesn't want anything to slow my recovery."

"I was really hoping you could come with us."

"Me, too." Todd tried to sound cheerful. "But there's always next year. Don't have too much fun without me."

"You're probably lucky you're staying home. Egg and Binky have been doing some pretty serious bickering these days. Oh! I almost forgot to tell you. We asked Ruth if she'd like to come on the retreat."

"Is she going?"

"I think so. She says she doesn't do well in big crowds, but we'll make it as easy for her as we can."

"I hope she has fun, and gets to know some of the gang. Say, what did you mean by Egg and Binky doing some 'serious bickering'? They're always bickering, aren't they?"

"Oh, it's those new glasses of Binky's."

"They look nice, don't they?"

"That's what I keep telling her. Everyone says the same thing, except Egg. Every time he calls her 'Four Eyes,' she explodes."

"Of course. And every time she explodes, Egg gets a big charge out of it."

"I spend half my time calming Binky down and the other half telling Egg to leave her alone."

"As long as she reacts that way, he's going to keep teasing her."

"Maybe you should tell her that, Todd."

Todd burst into laughter. "Binky? Listen to me?"

"Maybe Peggy could do it," Lexi mused. "Binky has a lot of respect for her."

"I suppose it's worth a try. By the way," Todd said, "Jennifer was here tonight. She still needs help with her algebra."

"I haven't heard much about that lately," Lexi said. "How's it going?"

"She's still frustrated, but I think she's going to get a grip on it. Her teacher is planning to set up a math lab for the students who are having trouble. He told Jennifer that if she came every day and got extra help, he could almost guarantee that she'd pass the class."

"That's good news."

"Better yet, Jennifer's getting some other help. Matt Windsor is tutoring her."

"Great! Matt's a math whiz! Once he finally buckled down on his studies, he started getting straight A's in math."

"It seems like Jennifer is really looking for ways to get through the class, instead of just complaining about it. With tutoring and the math labs, I think she'll make it. I hope she and Matt don't have a disagreement and break up before she gets her grade!"

"It wouldn't be the first time," Lexi answered, crossing her feet and running her finger over the pattern on her leggings. "The Emerald Tones got together today. We have several new songs to go over. Mrs. Waverly said she's anxious for you to come back."

"I asked the doctor about that too. He said it wouldn't be too long. I think he's being too cautious about extracurricular activities, but Mom says I have to do *exactly* what he says."

"Todd?" Lexi could hear Mrs. Winston calling him in the background. "Are you still on the telephone?"

"It's time to do my physical therapy exercises."

"Talk to you later," Lexi said cheerfully.

"Bye, Lex."

Lexi set the phone down on her night stand and glanced at the clock. Suddenly her bedroom door flew open.

"Are you going to tuck me in tonight, Lexi?" Ben was wearing his favorite pajamas, printed with a car motif, and a bright red and blue bathrobe. Still damp from his bath, his hair was spiked. "Can we read?"

"What? I already read you three books tonight."

Ben smiled slyly. "I thought you forgot."

"Sorry, buddy. I'm not that easily fooled. We'll read again tomorrow, okay?"

Lexi took Ben's hand and walked him to his bedroom. Ben crawled under the covers and pulled them up to his chin. Then he folded his hands and asked sweetly, "Are we going to say our prayers together, Lexi?"

"Of course. You start."

"Dear God," Ben began solemnly, "thanks for my sister, Lexi, and my mom and dad, and all my friends at the Academy. And thanks for my bunny rabbit and my toys, and bless all my friends. Bless Todd and Egg and Binky, Peggy, and Jennifer. Oh, yeah, and God? Can you help me get a part in the Christmas play? Thanks. Good night! Amen."

Lexi believed she could go to God with any request, whether it be a part in the Christmas play, a broken friendship that needed healing, or a concern about school. Ben had learned the same simple trust.

"Oh, yeah, God, I almost forgot." Ben bolted to a sitting position. "Bless Binky and her new glasses. She looks really pretty in them. Make her like them, God. Okay? Amen."

Lexi added a prayer of her own—for Ruth Miller, asking that Ruth be accepted by the other students at Cedar River. When she finished, she tucked the quilts in around Ben and kissed him gently on the forehead.

"Good night, sweet boy. See you in the morning."

———

"I'm glad I don't have a class this hour." Lexi and Egg entered the library together.

"Me too. I have to return this book." Egg held a large volume under his arm. "The librarian's been after me for two days. I keep forgetting it in my locker."

"Binky, Jennifer, and I are going to study," Lexi told him. "Want to join us?"

"Why not? Maybe I can teach you girls a thing or two."

Lexi gave him a playful look. "Maybe we can teach *you* something."

"You're no fun to tease, Lexi. You never get upset."

"You mean, like your sister?"

Egg looked a little embarrassed. "It's almost too easy to get Binky riled. There's no challenge in it anymore."

"It might be nice if you'd just leave her alone for a change. I thought you two were going to turn over a new leaf."

"If I didn't tease her once in a while, she'd think I didn't like her anymore," Egg explained. "You know, we tried acting civilized for a while and it felt . . . empty. Sounds crazy, but we show our feelings for each other by teasing and arguing."

"I hate to admit it," Lexi said, "but I believe you. Binky can't live with you and she can't live without you."

Just then the object of their conversation bolted into the library, flushed and upset.

"Dead meat! That's what I am. Dead meat." Binky flung herself into a chair.

The librarian frowned slightly at her, but didn't say anything.

"Dead meat," Binky repeated in a whisper. "What am I going to do?"

"Why, what happened?" Lexi asked.

"You haven't been in school long enough today to flunk any tests," Egg reasoned.

"Flunking a test is nothing, Egg. Look at this."

Binky pulled her new glasses out of her pocket—in two pieces.

"Binky, they're broken!" Lexi exclaimed.

"You've got that right." Binky put her head on her arm and groaned. "I can't believe I've broken my brand-new glasses. Mom and Dad are going to be furious."

"How did it happen, Bink?" Egg looked almost sympathetic.

"Brian James and I sort of collided," Binky explained. "He was bending down to get something from the bottom of his locker. I guess he didn't see I was already on the floor trying to find my pen. I came up just as he came down. I heard a crack, and my glasses slid right off my face. When I picked them up, the bow came off in my hand."

"You know why it happened, don't you?" Egg said.

"What do you mean? Brian James and I cracked heads."

"That's just your excuse."

"My *excuse*? That's what happened, Egg!" Binky's eyes narrowed.

"You broke your glasses because you subconsciously hate them."

"What? You're studying psychology now? I accidentally broke my glasses, and you're saying it's because I hate them? You're weird, Egg. Do you know that?" she said with scorn.

"You can't accept the fact that you have to wear glasses. Your subconscious mind set you up to get them broken. I *know* that's it."

"Uh, Egg, what was that book you just returned?" Lexi asked.

"A book on psychology. Why?"

"Just wondering," Lexi said with a smile. "I knew this little lecture had to be coming from somewhere."

Lexi examined Binky's glasses carefully. "I don't think it's as bad as it looks."

"They're broken, Lexi. That's all there is to it," Binky whimpered.

"Not exactly. Look." Lexi showed Binky where the little screw holding the bow to the frame had fallen out. "The screw shouldn't be hard to replace. The optical shop will probably replace it for you without charge."

"Well, that's not all. Look at this." Binky placed her glasses on her nose. One side was higher on one side than the other."

Lexi stifled a chuckle. "That can be fixed, too. They just need a little adjustment."

"I haven't even cleaned the lenses yet, and I break the frames! My mother's going to kill me!"

"Binky, you *are* in serious trouble." Egg eyed her sternly from across the table. "Big trouble."

Binky gave Egg a swift kick beneath the table. He was only saved from further punishment by Jennifer's arrival.

Egg scowled. "Now it'll be three against one."

"What are you talking about, Egg?" Jennifer sat down next to him. "I've had it. I've absolutely had it. I cannot memorize the formulas in algebra, let alone apply them. Who cares, anyway, if the product of two consecutive integers is forty-eight? I never should have listened to my advisor. I knew I'd never understand this stuff." She cast a forlorn look at her friends. "I think I'll have to drop out of school."

"Over algebra?" Egg looked incredulous.

"Jennifer, you can't be serious," Lexi said calmly.

"Would you really drop out of school because of one subject?" Binky asked.

"Binky," Egg said in a condescending tone, "people say things they don't mean literally. For instance, you just said you were dead meat. You know you aren't. You might get a lecture from Mom, but you won't be dead meat."

Binky gave Egg an icy look and turned to her friends.

"Have you seen Matt today, Jennifer?" Lexi asked. "Isn't he going to tutor you?"

"He started, but it's hopeless. I know it's hopeless."

"The only thing that's hopeless, Jennifer, is your attitude."

Jennifer looked startled at Lexi's tone of voice.

"You can do it. Todd says you're doing better. And Matt can help you. People in the math lab will help you, too. You just have to keep at it, Jennifer. You don't have an algebra problem, you have an *attitude* problem." Lexi surprised herself at her boldness in the way she spoke to Jennifer.

"Dropping out of school never solves anything. Who's waging this battle, anyway, you or a dumb algebra problem?"

Egg rose from his seat and quietly headed for the door. "I'll let you girls sweat it out. And by the way, Jennifer, I hope you win the battle." He gave Jennifer a smile and disappeared through the door.

Jennifer whistled. "I didn't know Egg could be so sweet. And you, Lexi, you really laid into me. I haven't heard you talk like that for ages."

"You haven't been so discouraged in ages."

"True. And I suppose I deserved it." Jennifer

opened her algebra book and glared at the pages. "A is for attitude, right? Look out quadratic equations. I'm going to have such a good attitude, I'll love you to death."

The girls' giggles caused the librarian to look sternly in their direction again.

"Time to get out of here," Binky muttered.

Out in the hallway, Jennifer leaned against the wall and closed her eyes. "I know one thing for sure," she said dreamily. "I'm ready to go on that youth retreat. I definitely need a change of pace."

"Me too!" Binky agreed.

"I think we're all ready to get away for the weekend," Lexi said, smiling at her friends.

Chapter Ten

The church doors were jammed with young people bringing in their sleeping bags and suitcases.

"Watch it, Egg. We can't both go through this door at the same time," Binky yelped. "We'll get stuck. Move your sleeping bag! There now . . . Ooof." Binky popped into the foyer of the church.

Egg stumbled in after her. Each carried a huge green sleeping bag that had seen many years of camping use. Their large suitcases showed signs of considerable wear and tear also.

Binky wore a thick jacket with matching wool knit hat and scarf. Egg looked like a lumberjack in blue jeans, red and black buffalo plaid shirt, and thick-soled boots.

"How long are you two planning to be gone?" Lexi asked, laughing at the pair. "A week? A month?"

"Very funny," Binky kicked at the suitcase with her toe. "I couldn't find a smaller bag. Then, after Egg had filled his own suitcase, he stuffed a bunch of junk in mine."

Lexi eyed Egg's huge bag. "You needed more than you could carry in that thing?"

"I've never been to a retreat. We're going to be roughing it, aren't we? I just packed a few things

97

necessary for a comfortable night."

"Food," Binky corrected. "Lots of food."

"But Pastor Lake said there would be plenty of food provided," Lexi commented.

"What if it doesn't show up? We may have to go out and hunt for rabbit and deer, butcher it ourselves and grill it over a campfire."

"That's highly unlikely, Egg. Pastor Lake mentioned pizza, I think."

He grinned. "I know that, but it might be hard to find enough marshmallows and chocolate bars for s'mores." He pointed to Binky's suitcase. "I've got enough in there to feed the whole group."

"That isn't all he's got, Lexi."

Egg gave his sister a warning glance. She ignored him. "He's got a jug of water, matches, books, games, and . . ." Binky lowered her voice theatrically, "toilet paper."

"Shut up, Binky! You weren't supposed to tell anyone about that," Egg growled.

Lexi giggled.

"You never know what you might need in the wilderness. You may be thanking me when this weekend is over, Binky."

Lexi was glad Jennifer and Peggy had just arrived.

"This is so embarrassing," Jennifer said. "I can't stand it. Look at my sleeping bag."

"It's got puppies and kittens on it," Binky said, laughing.

"I know. It's the one I had when I was little. We looked all over the house but couldn't find my other sleeping bag, so Mom made me bring this. I feel like a total nerd."

"What a cute little sleeping bag," Tim chirped as he sauntered by. "That will be cozy in the woods."

"Be quiet, Tim Anders. Maybe I happen to like kittens and puppies."

"What's the trouble?" Pastor Lake came up to them.

"Tim doesn't like my sleeping bag," Jennifer said sheepishly.

Pastor Lake chuckled. "It looks like it'll work all right."

"You don't like it either?"

"I didn't say that. I think it's rather interesting. Everyone carries equipment typical of their own personality or style."

Lexi looked around the room. Tim's sleeping bag was a standard one, but a large camera was slung across the pack. That was appropriate, considering Tim was photographer for the *River Review*. Matt Windsor's duffle bag was made of black leather that matched his jacket. Anna Marie Arnold's canvas overnight bag was bulging at the seams; she liked several changes of clothes. Tressa and Gina Williams were carrying bright-colored designer travel cases. Minda Hannaford's sleeping bag appeared to be brand new. Lexi guessed that Minda had never had the opportunity—or desire—to use one before now.

"You're right, Pastor Lake," Lexi commented. "Everyone's gear is a little different, and . . . typical."

"Exactly. And before this retreat is over, I hope all of you will get to know each other a little better—and understand each other more."

"That sounds like work," Binky said. She cast a glance at her brother. "Besides, I've been trying to understand Egg for my entire life and I haven't solved the puzzle yet."

Before Pastor Lake could respond to Binky's dilemma, the church doors flew open and the bus driver entered, rubbing his hands together against the early morning chill. "The bus is ready and waiting!"

Ruth Miller slipped in past the driver. She stood off to one side as Pastor Lake called the group to attention.

"I'm glad all of you could come. We can look forward to a time of fun and fellowship. Let's all relax and enjoy this weekend together. I hope you will make an effort to get to know someone that you didn't know before. For those of you who may be worrying about hours of Bible study and prayer, I want to put your mind at ease. We will have some Bible study and prayer, of course, but I'm pretty sure you will enjoy it more than you think. Let's keep an open mind and heart. We'll also have plenty of music, games, food and fellowship. Everything we do can be done for the glory of God. He is honored in our play as well as in our worship. Let's pause now for a word of prayer.

"Dear Heavenly Father, be with us as we embark upon this adventure together. Bless our fun, our fellowship, our friendship. Give us the gifts of discernment, awareness, compassion, and joy. May friendships be deepened this weekend, Lord, and our relationship with you strengthened. This we ask in the name of Jesus Christ. Amen."

Pastor Lake looked up and smiled at Ruth. "And I'd like to express an especially hearty welcome to the newcomer to our group."

Ruth blushed deeply. Lexi slipped quickly to her side. She took Ruth's cold hand in her own and squeezed it.

"I'm glad you're here," Lexi whispered. "It's going to be fun." Lexi could feel Ruth relax as attention was drawn away from her to the task at hand, that of packing the luggage into the bus.

"I'm sorry I'm late," Ruth said softly. "It took my aunt a while to get everything together."

"You're not really late. You're just on time."

"I'm still not sure I should be going," Ruth said hesitantly. "It won't be easy with . . . you know."

"You'll be fine," Lexi assured her. "Will you sit with me on the bus?"

Ruth's expression brightened. "Of course." She picked up her luggage and moved toward the door. After handing her gear to Pastor Lake, Ruth climbed onto the bus after Lexi.

"Save seats for us!" Binky yelled.

"No saving," Tim retorted. "Every man for himself."

"Then get moving, Tim. You're too slow."

The good-natured ribbing continued as Lexi and Ruth found seats. Soon Jennifer, Peggy, Binky and Egg joined them.

When Anna Marie Arnold came alone down the aisle, Egg stood up. "Would you like to sit here with Binky? I'll go in back."

"Sure, Egg. Thanks."

Egg gave his sister a warning glance. "Don't touch anything," he muttered under his breath. "And whatever you do, don't eat my food."

"As if I'd want your food," Binky answered, disgust written on her face.

"Anna Marie, have you met Ruth Miller?" Jennifer introduced the girls to each other.

Before long, conversation was drowned out by the

singing of some rousing choruses. Lexi was glad
Ruth had come. She would see what a great youth
group they had, and maybe decide to come regularly
to their meetings.

"I've got a joke," Tim announced, when the singing had died down. He stood in the middle of the
aisle, swaying back and forth with the motion of the
bus. "How can you tell when Egg McNaughton has
been using your computer?" He paused a moment
while several threw out their guesses. "You can see
the eraser crumbs on your computer screen."

Groans and moans erupted throughout the
crowded bus.

The tips of Egg's ears were pink, but he was grinning widely. "I've got a joke, too.

"Why does it take Tim so long to make chocolate
chip cookies?"

"I didn't know he knew how to make them," someone commented.

"Because it takes so long to peel the M&Ms!"

After about fifteen minutes of old jokes, Pastor
Lake whistled loudly to get everyone's attention.
"How about a quick game of Bible Trivia?"

"That sounds too much like work," someone
moaned.

"You have to think when you play that," someone
else said.

"We need to put our brilliant minds to good use,"
Pastor Lake countered. "The left side of the bus
against the right. Okay?"

"Let's go for it," Brian James yelled from the back
of the bus.

"In Matthew 18, a shepherd lost one of his sheep.

How many did he leave behind to look for the one
that had strayed?"

"Ninety-nine!"

"Right. Who must we be like in order to enter the
kingdom of heaven?"

"A little child!"

"Good. In Matthew 6, we are told not to worry
about what we will eat or drink, or what we will wear.
What examples are given of God's creation that are
not concerned with these things?"

"The birds of the air."

"The flowers of the field."

"Very good. When we get to the retreat center,
we'll pull out the hard questions."

After a while, everyone was quiet, contemplating
the weekend ahead. Lexi turned to Ruth.

"Ruth, is there something wrong?"

"I just realized I forgot my alarm clock," she said,
looking dismayed.

"That's no big deal. You won't need it."

"What if I don't wake up?"

"With all the commotion that will be going on?
How could you sleep through . . ." Lexi stopped mid-
sentence. All the commotion in the world wouldn't
wake Ruth without her hearing aids.

"I could sleep all morning." Tears sprang to
Ruth's eyes. "What if everyone were laughing at me
while I slept and I didn't know it."

"Oh, Ruth. No one would do that," Lexi assured
her. "None of us . . ." Lexi bit her lip. Well, maybe
the Hi-Fives. She wouldn't put anything past them.

"Don't worry about it, Ruth. I'll wake you when
I get up. I promise. I hope I don't wake up too early
for you."

Ruth looked relieved. "Wake me anytime. Just don't let me lie there with my mouth open, snoring away while everyone stares at me."

Lexi giggled. "I'm sure it's not *that* bad."

"Maybe not. But I'm very self-conscious about such things."

Lexi felt Ruth's pain. She knew how easy it was for people to tease a person like Ruth, or Lexi's brother, Ben. Lexi noticed that many times people spoke to Ben more loudly than necessary, assuming that because he had Down's syndrome, his hearing was defective too. Maybe the reverse was thought of Ruth. Because she was deaf, people may assume her mind wasn't sound.

"Don't worry about a thing," Lexi assured her friend. "We'll get up together. And if I don't hear *my* alarm, they'll have two of us to laugh at." Lexi felt like crying at Ruth's grateful smile.

"Look!" someone yelled. "The sign for Honeyford Retreat Center—one mile."

Whistles and shouts were heard throughout the bus. Egg and Binky began bickering over Binky's missing gloves.

"We're getting there in the nick of time," Jennifer confided to Peggy. "Egg and Binky are arguing again."

"Don't they like each other?" Ruth asked.

"Binky and Egg are crazy about each other," Lexi said. "They just like to bicker."

"It's hard to explain," Jennifer added. "But they aren't happy unless they're at each other's throats."

The bus rumbled to a halt in the driveway of a large church tucked away in the trees, on a cliff overlooking a small lake.

"Oooohh, how pretty!" Binky enthused.

"What about the congregation? Will they be here on Sunday?" someone wondered aloud.

"When the congregation got too small to afford upkeep on the building, they joined another congregation a few miles from here and donated their church as a youth retreat," Pastor Lake explained. "We have it to ourselves."

"I can hardly wait!"

"This is going to be great!"

Everyone seemed to tumble out of the bus at once, gather their gear, and head toward the old church.

"Wow, it's nice in here!" Brian said as he entered the lower level. Sliding glass doors led out to a narrow path that descended to the lake.

"This is where we'll have our meals and our Bible studies," Pastor Lake explained, indicating the long tables.

The room was large and cozy. Sofas and easy chairs were placed in a semi-circle facing a massive stone fireplace.

"The girls will sleep down here," Pastor Lake continued. "The guys get the second floor, the former sanctuary. There are a few cots up there. We'll have to draw straws; there aren't enough for everyone. I'll join you fellows."

"Do the girls get a chaperon, too?" Tim asked.

Pastor Lake chuckled. "I guess you could call her that. I've invited a friend of mine, Emily Warren, to join us for the evening. She'll sleep down here with the girls."

"Ha! You thought you'd get by without a chaperon!" Egg spoke loudly, pointing at Binky.

"Well, we certainly don't need one," Binky retorted. "You boys probably need more than one."

Egg sputtered as Pastor Lake instructed the boys to carry their gear upstairs. Not anxious to hang around doing nothing, the boys disappeared in a flash, leaving the girls to explore their quarters.

"I like it here," Jennifer said, flopping down on a comfortable sofa. "I could get used to this life."

"I'm used to it already," Binky said cheerfully. "I claim this other couch for my bed!"

"There are plenty of cots in the corner," Lexi said. "With our sleeping bags they won't be too bad."

The girls rushed to claim their cots and arrange them for the night. By the time they were organized, the boys had returned.

Without comment, Pastor Lake posted an agenda on the bulletin board near the door.

"First we go on a nature hike," Egg read aloud. "Then we have a Bible study, and after that a softball game. After supper we're going to do some singing and have devotions together." He glanced at his watch. "We'd better get busy if we're going to fit all that in today."

"My thoughts exactly," said Pastor Lake. "Let's be on our way."

Chapter Eleven

"Nature hike? Who ever heard of anything as boring as a nature hike? What's to see anyway? Grass and dirt, sky and trees," Minda mumbled under her breath.

"And bugs. You forgot to mention the bugs," Tressa added.

"Will you two be quiet?" Jennifer said. "All you've done is complain for the last forty-five minutes."

"That's because all we've been doing is *walking* for the last forty-five minutes. I'm getting a little weary of it," Minda countered.

"Shhhh, you're scaring the squirrels," Binky reprimanded.

"Yeah, right. The squirrels are scaring me is more like it," Tressa answered.

"Why do we have to do this anyway?" Minda moaned. "Couldn't he have rented a video so we could stay inside, instead of wandering around out here in the mud and grime?"

"You don't get it, do you, Minda? We're supposed to be appreciating the beauty of God's creation. Don't you see how everything harmonizes with every other thing and fits together for our enjoyment? You can hardly see that sitting in front of a television set watching a video," Jennifer explained.

"I still think a video would be a whole lot easier than this," Minda muttered.

Pastor Lake was quite knowledgeable of the area. He identified a number of birds and plants, pointed out a fox's den, and a mother deer and her doe camouflaged among the trees. He also knew what kinds of fish could be caught in the small lake.

Peggy drew a deep breath of the fresh air. "It's great out here, isn't it? No traffic, no telephones, no homework . . ."

"No television or radio," Binky added. "This must be how God intended it should be."

"No pollution," Jennifer rejoined, "no motorcycles with noisy mufflers . . ."

"God has planned the very best for us and for the universe," Pastor Lake said quietly, coming up behind the girls. "It's too bad we don't always appreciate His creation. We are, as a rule, very ungrateful children."

"We do try sometimes, though." Binky launched into the story of Egg's campaign to put a brick in every toilet and save the environment. By the time she was finished, Pastor Lake was laughing hysterically.

"Good for you," he said. "I like young people with spirit. That's a great story."

Minda had a pouty look on her face. She didn't like being left out of a conversation. "Can we go back now?" she asked grumpily. "My feet are killing me."

No wonder, Lexi thought. Minda had insisted on wearing fashion boots instead of hiking shoes.

"Good idea, Minda," Pastor Lake said kindly. "My feet are beginning to ache, too. Maybe we should all sit down in the clearing up ahead and have our Bible study right out here in the open."

"That's not quite what I meant . . ." Minda began, but apparently decided to save her negative comments. She could hardly criticize Pastor Lake after he'd so readily acknowledged her complaint.

Everyone sat down on rocks and logs, forming a circle as best they could. Most were glad for the chance to rest, but no one quite knew what to expect. Pastor Lake was always full of surprises.

"I want each of you to think awhile about a topic you would like discussed. After everyone has given their ideas, we'll choose a subject that relates the most directly to all of us."

"I don't get it," Tressa complained.

"What's important to you, Tressa?" Pastor Lake asked. "Is there something you think about often, and need some answers to?"

"I think about shopping a lot!" Tressa said with a grin. "But I suppose you mean more important things . . . I think about my friends, about being popular . . . that sort of stuff."

"Friendship. Making and keeping friends. Good suggestion, Tressa."

Tressa seemed startled that Pastor Lake had thought her topic viable.

"I think it's hard to pray," Tim said frankly. "When things are going well it's no problem. But when things aren't going so well I feel guilty coming to God. It's like I'm begging or something."

"I think about school," Jennifer said quietly. "I'm always afraid I'm going to flunk out. I have this fear that no matter how hard I study, I'll get things mixed up on tests. Even knowing the teachers will help me doesn't make me feel any better."

Lexi was amazed at the topics for discussions that came up. To her, it was apparent that the concerns, doubts, fears, and questions were coming straight from everyone's heart.

"I worry about being laughed at," Ruth said quietly. "I know I miss what's being said sometimes. I don't like feeling like a fool."

"I think about what God wants me to do with my life," Egg admitted. "Does He want me to go to college? If so, where? What should be my major? I don't want to make any mistakes."

As each one spoke in turn, Lexi felt as though she were seeing and hearing some of them for the first time. It seemed odd to her that she could know people for more than a year and not know their deepest concerns.

When everyone had spoken, Pastor Lake looked around the circle. His expression was one of affection and concern. "You've all shared more than I'd hoped," he said, "and it's going to be impossible to choose one subject over another, because they're all good, and most are of interest to many of you. But I'm hearing one underlying theme—worry."

"I'm not worried!" Egg protested. "It's just that . . . well, maybe I am a little worried."

"Worry is almost a prerequisite to being a teenager," Pastor Lake said, smiling. "You have so many things to think about, so many adjustments to make—grade requirements in school, acceptance among your peers, excelling in sports, learning to be responsible, independent; what to do with your future—dating, marriage, college. Some teens have the added worry of their parents' troubled or failed marriage, financial difficulties in the family, sibling rivalry. Probably the most difficult fact is that many of the things you worry about are things over which you have no control."

Everyone nodded, showing their unanimous consent to what Pastor Lake was saying.

"Interestingly, the Bible has quite a bit to say about worry. God must have known we would face a lot of worry in our life on earth. He has given us a lot of advice on how to handle it. As we talk about the things that worry us, and what the Bible has to say about it, I'd like each of you to apply God's Word to your own particular situation."

Pastor Lake opened his small Bible and began to read. "In Matthew 6:25–34 it says,

> Therefore I tell you, do not worry about your life, what you will eat or drink; or about your body, what you will wear. Is not life more important than food, and the body more important than clothes? Look at the birds of the air; they do not sow or reap or store away in barns, and yet your heavenly Father feeds them. Are you not much more valuable than they? Who of you by worrying can add a single hour to his life.
>
> And why do you worry about clothes? See how the lilies of the field grow. They do not labor or spin. Yet I tell you that not even Solomon in all his splendor was dressed like one of these. If that is how God clothes the grass of the field, which is here today and tomorrow is thrown into the fire, will he not much more clothe you, O you of little faith? So do not worry, saying, "What shall we eat?" or "What shall we drink?" or "What shall we wear?" For the pagans run after all these things,

and your heavenly Father knows that you need them. But seek first his kingdom and his righteousness, and all these things will be given to you as well. Therefore do not worry about tomorrow, for tomorrow will worry about itself. Each day has enough trouble of its own.

Everyone was silent, pondering the words. Then Egg mumbled, "It's not as easy as it sounds!"

Pastor Lake smiled. "You're absolutely right, Egg. Trusting is often the hardest job of all. But if we believe that God is in control of every situation, then we know we aren't alone. We've got help. Romans 8:28 says, 'In all things God works for the good of those who love him.' There's another way to look at it too: 'Cast all your anxiety on him because he cares for you.' That's 1 Peter 5:7."

"Sounds like a great idea!" Tim blurted. "I'd love to give someone my problems!"

"That's exactly what God invites you to do. He wants you to live each day for itself and not worry about what might happen next. You can tell God, 'I'm worried about my algebra test, or making friends, or where I should go to college. I give that worry to you. Please take it, and help me with the answer.' "

"And He will?"

"He's done it for me." Pastor Lake answered matter-of-factly. "It might sound a little presumptuous to anyone who hasn't experienced it, but when I've turned my concerns over to God, He's given me a peace of mind that's impossible to explain. He's made me feel . . . quiet . . . inside, like I couldn't worry about that particular problem even if I wanted to. When I knew I was no longer alone with my problem, it didn't seem like such a big deal anymore.

"Sometimes He'll show me what my next step

should be. A new, fresh idea might pop into my head that I'd never considered before, or I begin to realize what's important and what's not. God wants us to enjoy each day. He'll give you what you need to get through it. What you couldn't accomplish alone, the two of you can manage together."

"You make it sound like God's your . . . best friend . . . or something," Minda said.

"He is. And He can be yours, too."

Pastor Lake could see that some in the group were getting restless. "Maybe this is enough discussion for now."

"These aren't the most comfortable chairs," Egg admitted. His was a triangular-shaped rock. Suddenly a strange expression came over Egg's features.

"Egg, are you all right?" Pastor Lake asked.

Egg began to shake one leg violently. Then he stiffened and slid to the ground.

"What's wrong with him?" someone asked.

Pastor Lake hurried to his side as Egg writhed on the ground, clawing at his pant leg.

"He's having some kind of a fit!" Tim shouted.

"Egg, stop it!" Binky demanded.

Pastor Lake knelt down and asked, "Can you tell me what's wrong, Egg?"

After another dramatic twitching of his leg, Egg answered sheepishly, "It's a m . . . m . . . mouse. There's a mouse in my pants," he said stiffly.

As everyone watched, wide-eyed, a tiny gray field mouse darted out of Egg's jeans and into a clump of grass. Egg gave a wrenching sigh and collapsed. "It . . . it tickled something awful."

Everyone burst out laughing, and Binky lunged for her brother's throat. "You scared me half to death!

I thought you were dying! A mouse in your pants! I can't believe it."

"How would you like it, Binky? Those sticky little feet and scratchy tail running up and down your leg!" Egg was as red as a beet.

"Oh, gross! How awful!"

Pastor Lake was having a hard time keeping a straight face.

"How about a game of softball?" he suggested, offering Egg a hand.

"Sure!"

"Sounds great!"

"Where can we play?"

"There's a clearing on the other side of the retreat center," Pastor Lake explained. "Last one there is bat boy."

The rush was on. By the time Lexi and Ruth reached the clearing, the boys were already choosing sides. Lexi saw Ruth's terrified expression.

"What's wrong?" Lexi asked.

"I can't play softball. I don't know how."

"You mean you've never played before?" Binky asked, incredulous.

"No. I've seen it played," Ruth said meekly, "but I've never played myself."

"All you have to do is hit the ball with the bat and run around the bases," Binky said simply.

"But what if I don't hit the ball?"

"That just makes it easier," Binky said with a shrug. "If you don't hit the ball you don't have to run the bases."

Egg was a team captain. He quickly caught on to Lexi's worried look and announced loudly, "I pick Ruth Miller for my team."

Ruth hesitated, but Lexi gave her a gentle shove. "Go on; you'll do fine."

The teams were soon equally drawn. Of the girls, Lexi, Ruth, Minda, and Jennifer were on Egg's team; Gina, Binky, Anna Marie, and Tressa on the opposing team. Egg lost the flip of the coin, and his team started out in the field.

"We're never going to win. We're just never going to win," Minda announced.

"How can you say that?" Egg said in a disgusted tone. "We haven't even started to play yet."

"Look at our team. We're going to be lousy."

Lexi studied the mix of boys and girls. "I don't see why."

"Well, for one thing, we have the deaf girl with us," Minda said, not bothering to keep her voice down.

"Be quiet!" Jennifer whispered fiercely. "You'll hurt her feelings."

"She can't hear anyway. Those big, ugly hearing aids can't help that much. Maybe if we stick her in the outfield behind third base . . ."

"Minda, stop that." Lexi was angry. "Just because she has trouble hearing doesn't mean she can't learn to play ball."

"*Learn* is the operative word here, isn't it?" Minda retorted. "She doesn't know how. She's not going to catch on that quick, and we're going to lose. That's all there is to it." Minda stomped off in a huff.

From the corner of her eye, Lexi saw Ruth's shoulders droop. "I don't think I feel like playing, anyway," Ruth murmured. "Maybe I'll just go inside."

"No way! You aren't going to let some thoughtless

thing Minda said stop you from having a good time."

"But if I'm here, *she* won't have a good time," Ruth pointed out.

"She will if we win," Lexi grinned slyly. "How's your eye/hand coordination?"

"Pretty good, I guess. I'm good at racquetball."

"Then we have nothing to worry about. Come on."

Lexi was right. In spite of Ruth's hearing impairment, there was nothing wrong with her hands and legs. She caught three pop flies and didn't strike-out once, which was more than you could say for Minda. At the end of nine innings, Egg's team came out on top by one run.

"We did it, we did it! We won! Way to go team!" Jennifer yelled.

Minda stared blankly at her teammates. She crossed her arms tightly over her chest and her lower lip protruded in a pout.

"What's wrong with *you*, Minda?" Egg asked. "Aren't you happy we won? Even though you nearly blew the game for us about six times."

"Oh, shut up!"

"Well, if Ruth hadn't played, we would have been the losers."

"I guess handicapped people have to be good at something," Minda muttered.

"I wish you would stop calling Ruth handicapped, Minda," Lexi said. "If she hadn't turned out to be such a great softball player, we'd be doing dishes tonight. The losing team does them, you know."

Minda merely scowled.

"That's right," Egg affirmed. "That reminds me, I'm getting hungry. What's for supper?"

Chapter Twelve

"I'm so starved I could eat a field mouse," Jennifer announced, snickering at Egg as she walked through the door of the retreat center.

"You might have to," Brian James said gloomily. "Pastor Lake just told us *we're* doing the cooking."

"All of us have to cook?"

"No, just us." Brian pointed to Tim and a few of the other guys on the losing team. "The rest of the losers have to do dishes."

"Can you cook?" Ruth asked.

"No, but I suppose now is a good time to learn."

Minda, Tressa, and Gina groaned simultaneously. "We're going to starve."

"Pastor Lake has all the ingredients for homemade pizzas and sloppy joes. The restaurant that was going to provide pizzas for us had some trouble with their ovens," Brian explained.

"Do the sloppy joes," Lexi suggested. "That's easy. All you have to do is fry the hamburger and—"

"Would you help us?" Brian's eyes lit up.

"Good try, Brian, but Lexi and her team get the night off." Pastor Lake stepped into the kitchen. "There's a recipe on the counter."

After considerable muttering and mumbling, the

sloppy joes were finally ready. By the time Lexi sat down at one of the long tables to eat, her stomach was complaining loudly.

"These aren't too bad," Jennifer said after she'd taken a big bite. "Not bad at all."

"They're a little . . . sweet, aren't they?" someone asked.

"Egg insisted we add brown sugar to the barbecue sauce," Tim explained. "He said his mother does it all the time."

Binky took a bite and savored the sweetness. "Mom does use a little brown sugar, but not this much."

Despite the sweet twist, the sloppy joe mix rapidly disappeared along with stacks of buns, several boxes of potato chips, and a case of sherbet, served in paper cups.

"I feel much better now." Jennifer sprawled across a couch and moaned contentedly. "In fact, I could take a nap."

"Me, too." Lexi yawned. She hadn't spent so much time outdoors in quite a while. The fresh air had made her sleepy.

"Oh no you don't, girls," Pastor Lake announced. "You haven't met your chaperon yet, and Emily won't arrive for another half hour. I'm surprised you want to go to sleep so early."

Jennifer groaned. "Why do we need a chaperon, Pastor Lake? What do you think we're going to do, anyway?"

Before he could answer, the sliding door opened, and a petite woman dressed in jeans and a bright jacket stepped inside. She had curly blonde hair that fell around her shoulders and blue eyes that sparkled unpretentiously.

"Hello everybody! I'm here."

Pastor Lake jumped to his feet. "Emily, you're early!" He put his arm around the young woman's shoulders and turned to the group. "I'd like all of you to meet Emily Warren. She's the youth director at the church near here that has taken over the managerial duties of the retreat center."

Emily rubbed her hands together. "As a former Bible camp counselor, retreats are one of my very favorite things. Have you been having fun so far?"

The answer was a resounding *yes.*

"Good. Then let's have some more!" Emily bent to open the case she'd carried in. "Am I the only one who brought a guitar?"

"Nope." Pastor Lake picked up his acoustic guitar.

Emily smiled at the intrigued group before her. "Is everybody ready to sing?'"

After they'd exhausted the musical requests, Pastor Lake turned to Ruth. "Do you have a Bible verse you'd like to share with us for tonight's devotions?"

"Yes, I do have one I'd like to read." Ruth picked up a Bible lying on the table and turned to the book of Mark.

"This is my favorite passage in the Bible because it contains so much hope—especially for someone like me. It tells me that, with God, anything is possible. You'll understand what I mean when you hear the verses." Ruth began to read:

> Then Jesus left the vicinity of Tyre and went through Sidon, down to the Sea of Galilee and into the region of the Decapolis. There some people brought to him a man who was deaf and could hardly talk, and they begged him to place

his hand on the man.

After he took him aside, away from the crowd, Jesus put his fingers into the man's ears. Then he spit and touched the man's tongue. He looked up to heaven and with a deep sigh said to him, *"Ephphatha!"* (which means, "Be opened!"). At this, the man's ears were opened, his tongue was loosened and he began to speak plainly.

Ruth's eyes were shining as she finished the passage. She, more than anyone, could identify with the man's great joy.

"Sometimes I imagine what it would be like to be healed," she murmured shyly. Then gathering courage, she continued, "I think about how powerful my Savior is and the miracles He can do. It makes me so thankful that I can turn to Him with my problems."

Pastor Lake nodded knowingly.

"Actually, sometimes I forget my hearing impairment is a problem. When others are busy *listening* to people, I'm *watching*. People can often hide their true feelings with their words, but not with their faces. Sometimes I *hear* much better than most people!"

After a few more words on the text from Pastor Lake, they had a time of prayer, and then everyone stood and stretched to work out the kinks in their aching, stiff bodies.

Binky curled up in the corner of a couch, struggling to stay awake. She murmured contentedly, "This day has been great!"

"And I know what would make it even greater!" Egg announced. "S'mores!"

Several joined Egg in front of the fireplace to roast the marshmallows. Others passed out the graham crackers and chocolate bars Egg had brought along. Soon everyone's hands were into making the delicious treat.

Egg was so intent on finishing off the marshmallows in the bag that he didn't see Tim sneak up behind him with a large pillow poised over his head. Egg ducked just as Tim roared "Pillow fight!" Others grabbed pillows and joined the foray.

Lexi and Binky crawled away from the confusion and settled themselves in a corner to watch.

"Can you believe my brother?" Binky moaned. "What a geek."

"Life would be very dull without Egg," Lexi reminded her.

"But much less embarrassing. First a mouse in his pants, now this."

"Looks like Egg's side is losing," Lexi commented. "Maybe we should help him out."

"Not me! I don't feel like getting banged in the head with anything. Not even a pillow."

"We don't have to join them to rescue Egg," Lexi said, standing up. "Anybody for a game of Ping-Pong?" she yelled.

Egg had perched himself on a chair, and as he turned to look at Lexi, he fell to the floor, landing on Tim and a pile of pillows.

"Cease fire! Cease fire!" Tim yelled, his voice muffled.

"Come on." Lexi pulled Binky to her feet. "We have to show these guys how to play Ping-Pong."

"I have to warn you," Binky said, grabbing Lexi's

arm. "My brother is even worse at Ping-Pong than he is at pillow fights."

After two hours, the boys finally retreated to the second floor. The girls got into their pajamas and settled cozily around the flickering fire. It was a good time for sharing confidences, thoughts, and dreams.

As usual, Minda dominated the conversation. She directed some pointed questions at Ruth.

"How did you get . . . that way?" Minda gestured uncomfortably.

"My mother had German measles when she was pregnant with me," Ruth explained.

"I didn't think that sort of thing could happen," Jennifer said.

"My mother thought she'd already had the measles," Ruth told them, "so she wasn't inoculated. She had a light rash, but no one thought much about it at the time. Then, when I was about six months old, my mom decided I wasn't responding to their voices as I should. When I began to speak, and said nothing more than *mama* and *dada,* they took me to an ear specialist. The doctor discovered the nerves in my ears were damaged."

"Couldn't they help you?" Tressa asked. "I thought doctors could do just about anything these days."

"There's no real cure for nerve deafness."

"That's why you weren't able to speak?"

"We learn to talk by hearing others talk. Because my hearing was so poor, I didn't learn to speak properly."

"How awful," Binky said sympathetically.

"I'm luckier than most," Ruth said. "People born with a hearing impairment fifty years ago didn't get much help. They had to learn to read lips and the expressions on people's faces. I consider myself lucky to have these hearing aids."

"Lucky!" Gina blurted. "I don't know if I'd call that lucky."

"My parents placed me in a school for deaf children. Because I didn't have much language of my own, I had to be taught. After some testing, they discovered I did have some hearing and that it could be helped with hearing aids. That way, I learned to understand how words should sound, and that's how I'm able to speak."

"Was it hard?" Anna Marie asked. Her eyes were filled with compassion.

"I guess. Imagine trying to figure out the difference between *beach* and *peach* when the lip movements are so similar. The English language is a lot harder to understand when you aren't able to hear. It takes more work. I think I missed out on a lot of fun as a child. There wasn't much time for play."

"What did you do for fun?" Tressa asked.

"I did a lot of reading and drawing, and playing the piano. Even though I couldn't really hear how well I was doing, I liked the idea of looking at a note and pressing the key for that note on the piano. If I pounded loud enough, it felt like I was really making music."

"Did you have many friends?" Binky asked.

"No, because I was hard to understand, and they were impatient with me. If I was playing the piano, drawing, or reading and I made a mistake, I could stop and go back over it. Kids don't have much patience. If they'd say something to me once and if I didn't get it, they'd give up on me."

"Sounds horrible to me," Minda muttered.

"Sometimes it was hard not to feel sorry for myself," Ruth admitted. "But my parents never let me mope for very long. They taught me to look at things in a positive way. It could have been worse. I could have been born completely deaf."

"All this stuff is really amazing," Minda admitted. "I don't understand why I never heard any of it before."

Binky leaned over to Lexi and whispered, "Because she's always thinking about herself."

Lexi nudged Binky. It was good to see that Minda was somewhat concerned about Ruth, and not so quick to make smart remarks that were harmful.

As the room grew quiet, Lexi stared into the fire. She felt warm and cozy. So far, the retreat had been wonderful. What could be in store for them tomorrow?

Chapter Thirteen

Lexi awoke to an ear-splitting screech. She rubbed her eyes to wipe away the stinging smoke that clouded them. *Am I dreaming?* she wondered. *Maybe those sloppy joes we had last night upset my stomach.* She buried her head deep into her pillow just as the smoke alarm on the wall went off again.

Hey! This is for real! Lexi sat bolt upright just as Pastor Lake came bounding down the stairs barefoot. Confused, she focused on his toes. She couldn't remember ever seeing a barefoot pastor before.

Finally, it occurred to Lexi that there must be a fire somewhere in the building.

"Wake up, girls! Let's get out of here! There's a fire in the building!" Pastor Lake moved from cot to cot rousing the girls. "Emily, help! We've got to get everyone out of here!"

Emily jumped to her feet and began herding the girls toward the door. "Girls! Move quickly!" she commanded.

Pastor Lake's voice was loud and authoritative. "I can't locate the fire; there's too much smoke in here. Just get out of the building."

Binky sat on her cot in an emotional heap. Lexi could hear her hysterical sobs from across the room.

"We're all going to die. We'll never all get out of here in time."

"Shut up, Binky!" Minda retorted. "Get off that stupid cot and move your body!"

"What about our stuff?"

"Leave the stuff. We've got to get out of here."

"Where's my brother?" Binky's voice took on a new note of panic. "Where's Egg? He must still be upstairs. We've got to—"

"Egg is fine. The boys are already outside," Pastor Lake called to her.

"Oh, I can't stand this!" Binky wailed. "I can hardly breathe!"

"Pull it together, Binky." Jennifer took Binky by the arm and steered her toward the doorway.

The girls were finally filing outside, clutching coats and blankets for warmth.

"How do you think the fire started?" Peggy asked, shivering in the cold darkness.

"I don't know. There's a lot of smoke in there," someone answered.

"Do you think the fireplace backed up?"

"Could have been the wiring. The place is pretty old."

"We're lucky the smoke alarms worked."

As everyone talked at once about the close call, Pastor Lake ushered the last stragglers out into the fresh air.

Emily announced loudly that she'd called the fire department. They'd be here soon.

"Let's count off, to be sure everyone is out," Pastor Lake said.

"One."

"Two."

"Three . . ." they numbered off in broken, frightened voices.

"Twenty-six," Tim was the last to speak.

Pastor Lake was visibly shaken. "There were twenty-seven of you on the bus."

Who is missing? Lexi thought hard.

"Ruth!" she gasped suddenly. "I was supposed to wake her! She doesn't wear her hearing aids at night."

Binky immediately began to sob uncontrollably. "Please, someone! We have to get her out of there!"

"Where was she sleeping?" Pastor Lake asked.

Peggy spoke up in a meek voice. "It was getting crowded, and Ruth decided to move her sleeping bag under one of the tables—she was back by the kitchen door."

"No wonder I missed her!" Pastor Lake took a deep breath and headed for the door again.

"You can't go back in now!" Emily urged.

"We can't leave Ruth in there, either," he retorted sharply as he entered the smoke-filled basement.

The wail of fire trucks could be hear in the distance as Pastor Lake disappeared inside. Several of the girls were sobbing softly; some just stared ahead with blank expressions. Binky clung to her brother for support.

Lexi had to stifle the urge to run and peer into the windows to see if she could spot Pastor Lake and Ruth. Common sense held her back. The building could burst into flames at any moment.

"Oh, God, please help them to get out safely!" she repeated over and over.

"It sure is taking a long time," someone said.

"Maybe someone else should go in after them," another suggested.

"Absolutely not!" Emily commanded. "Everyone remain where they are."

The seconds ticked by; they seemed like hours. Just as the headlights of the first fire truck could be seen dancing through the trees, Pastor Lake burst through the doorway, a wet towel around his face, and Ruth in his arms. She was coughing and choking as he stumbled into the night air.

Everyone rushed forward. "Back up!" Pastor Lake shouted. "She needs the fresh air."

Suddenly, firemen in large rubber boots and thick coats came crashing through the trees.

"Do you know where the fire originated?" one of them asked Pastor Lake.

"I have no idea. I woke up to the building filled with smoke. We just got everyone out."

"Good. Stand back, we'll take care of it from here. An ambulance is right behind us. The paramedics will take care of anyone who needs oxygen. You must have inhaled a lot of smoke."

Pastor Lake looked enormously relieved to have someone else in charge. He turned to the group at the edge of the clearing. "It's time we had a word of prayer."

"Now?" Tressa blurted, obviously embarrassed at Pastor Lake's suggestion.

"The best thing to do at a time like this is to pray." Pastor Lake dropped to his knees. "Dear Lord, bless these firemen and help them to find the source of the fire and extinguish it quickly. Thank you for keeping us all safe; your hand was obviously upon us tonight. Thank you in particular, Lord, for keeping Ruth safe.

Just as the shepherd was concerned for the lamb who was lost, you are concerned about each of your children. We praise you, Lord, for your protection and faithfulness. Amen."

All the girls were crying, and most of the boys had tears in their eyes. The terrifying experience was over, and only now were they beginning to realize the tragedy that had been averted.

"She could have died!" Binky wailed, pointing to Ruth, who was being examined by a paramedic. "All that stuff we talked about—knowing God, having Him as our best Friend—it all seems to . . . to make sense now!"

The impact of Binky's words obviously affected many in the group.

"It's true," Tressa murmured. "If Ruth had died, she would have been with God right now." She swallowed nervously. "If it had been *me . . .*" her voice broke and she whispered, "would I have gone to be with God?"

"For God loved the world so much that he gave his one and only Son, that whoever believes in him shall not perish but have eternal life," Pastor Lake quoted softly. "That means *everyone.* All we have to do is accept His promise and believe."

Tressa looked suddenly pale in the moonlight. "I guess that means we'd better not put off believing." No one said a word. They were all lost in their own thoughts of life, death, and eternity.

Nearly an hour passed before one of the firemen addressed the group huddled in the clearing. "The fire started in the chimney. It was fairly well contained, except for the smoke. We've opened all the windows to air the place out. I'm afraid you'll have a tough time getting the smoke smell out of your clothes and sleeping bags."

"We don't care about that," Tim said. "We can replace all that stuff. You can't replace people, and we're all safe. Thank God for that."

"I agree with you one hundred percent." The fireman smiled at Tim. "It's almost morning. Is there anything else we can do for you?"

Emily obviously knew the fireman, and stepped forward. "Yes. Could you please call the pastor of my church? Ask him if some of the congregation would be willing to serve breakfast to the young people before they start back. We'll pack up and head for the church."

"That shouldn't be any problem, Emily. I'll see that breakfast is served before eight o'clock."

"Thanks, Dan."

While Pastor Lake was talking to the other firemen, some of the boys ventured near the building.

"Is it all right to go inside, Pastor Lake?"

"I think so. Get your things together as quickly as possible and wait outside."

"I guess the retreat is over," one of the boys said sadly.

"I'm ready to go home," Peggy admitted.

"Me, too," Binky agreed.

"What an experience. We'll never forget this retreat!" Lexi said.

After salvaging what they could of their wet, sooty belongings, everyone loaded the luggage compartment of the bus and filed into their seats for the ride to Emily's church.

Lexi didn't have the energy to engage in conversation. She sank wearily into the seat next to Ruth and closed her eyes. She could hear a muffled sob from the back of the bus. Lexi turned to see that it was Minda.

"What's wrong with her?" Lexi asked.

Ruth looked at her blankly.

"Ruth, where are your hearing aids?"

"Someone must have stepped on them," Ruth said flatly. She opened her hand to show Lexi the broken bits of plastic that were all that remained of her connection to the world. Her eyes filled with tears. "I can't hear anything now."

"Ruth, I'm ... I'm *so* sorry," Lexi stammered, struggling for the right words.

The sobbing from the back of the bus grew louder. "Excuse me," Lexi mouthed the words, looking directly at Ruth.

Lexi slipped down the aisle toward Minda. "What's wrong?"

Tressa and Gina both shrugged. "She just started crying all of a sudden, and we can't get her to talk."

"Let me sit with her."

Gina stood up, and Lexi slid in beside Minda.

"It's all right, Minda," she comforted, placing an arm around the girl's shoulder. "It's all over. Everyone is safe."

Minda's eyes were bloodshot and tears stained her cheeks. "I ... I just realized ... for the first time ... what it means to be deaf," Minda stammered. "I never thought it was a big deal. I always thought Ruth was a little ... dumb, or something. I never realized how much it could affect her ... her *life*." Minda shuddered. "She could have *died* in there, Lexi. If the fire had been bigger, out of control, Pastor

Lake might not have gotten her out in time. I'm so sorry. I'm *so, so* sorry."

"But she got out, Minda. Ruth is fine."

"But I've been so cruel!" Minda wailed. "I haven't cared about her feelings!" A determined look came over Minda's face. "I have to apologize to her."

"Ruth's hearing aids were destroyed. She won't be able to hear you."

Minda looked incredulous. "Her hearing aids are gone?"

"She can get new ones, of course," Lexi soothed, "But for now, she is really at a loss."

Minda shook her head and repeated over and over, "Why, why was I so insensitive?"

After a huge breakfast at Emily's church, the women of the congregation who'd served them gave dry sweaters to some of the girls and bid them goodbye. It was a subdued group that traveled back home that morning. There was no singing or games, and very little conversation.

When everyone had pulled their gear out of the bus and entered the church, Pastor Lake spoke up, "Those of you who have cars can help drive the others home, but before you leave, let's take a few moments to talk about what happened. It's important—and healthy—to discuss our feelings."

The tired young people formed a large circle in the fellowship room and waited for Pastor Lake to return from his office. No one had much to say, not even Egg and Binky. Binky still clung to her brother as though he were a lifeline.

Pastor Lake joined the circle. "Does anyone have something they'd like to say?"

Minda spoke first, leading the rest toward healing, "I—I learned something from this," she began uncertainly.

"And what is that, Minda?" Pastor Lake asked.

"I'm never going to take my hearing for granted again." She looked directly at Ruth who sat across the circle from her.

"I've been really rotten to Ruth," Minda admitted. "I realized for the first time last night how bad things *could* be—and how *good* they actually are. I know Ruth can't understand everything I'm saying now, but as soon as she gets new hearing aids, I'm going to tell her how sorry I am for the way I treated her. And I'm never going to take my own hearing for granted again."

"I'm never going to take my *life* for granted again," Tim said next. "When I first woke up and it was dark and hard to breathe, I wondered if we were all going to die. I realized then that I'd taken everything in my life for granted. I'm going to quit complaining about life and start *living* it!"

"And I'm going to quit griping about algebra!" Jennifer said with a faint grin. "I realized this morning that my attitude *has to change.* You'll never hear me complain again about anything as silly as an algebra problem. Frankly, I'm glad I'm still around to figure the problems out!"

Chapter Fourteen

Lexi dragged her sleeping bag and suitcase into the house. The events of the last few hours had left her exhausted, both physically and emotionally. The realization that they could have lost Ruth in a fire because she hadn't heard their cries was an eye-opener to everyone.

"Hey, sleepyhead," Todd greeted Lexi. "You're sure home early." He was sitting on the couch with an open book on his lap. Benjamin was cuddled next to him, his head resting on Todd's shoulder.

"Todd's been reading to me," Ben announced proudly. "Three stories."

"What did they do to you at the retreat?" Todd asked. "You look terrible!"

"Thanks a lot." For the first time that morning, Lexi looked down at her dirty sweatshirt and soot-covered jeans. She could only imagine what her hair looked like.

"What happened?" Mrs. Leighton walked into the room. "Why are you back so early?"

"Didn't Pastor Lake call?"

"I don't think so. I'll bet you girls talked all night. Am I right, Lexi?"

A tall young man with a boyish grin stepped from behind Mrs. Leighton.

Lexi dropped her sleeping bag to the floor. "Harry Cramer! What in the world are you doing here?"

"I came to see you. Nice hairdo."

Harry was Binky's boyfriend, now a freshman in college. His hair looked longer than usual to Lexi, and she also noticed the familiar chip in his front tooth.

"Hey, it's a long story," she said, punching Harry in the arm. "You're taller than when you left home," Lexi said.

"Todd said the same thing."

"College food must be agreeing with you."

"That's doubtful. Maybe it's the midnight pizzas."

Ben interrupted to excuse himself from the room. "See you later, guys. I'm going to feed my rabbit."

"See you, Ben," Lexi said, ruffling her brother's hair. "Binky didn't mention you were coming home this weekend, Harry."

"That's because she didn't know. I was planning to surprise her. When I got here and called her place, I found out she and Egg were on a church retreat. Great surprise, huh? I'm here and she's somewhere else."

"Well, if Lexi's here, Binky must be around, too," Todd observed.

"Tell us about the retreat, dear," Lexi's mother said, looking a bit anxious.

Lexi groaned softly. "I don't even know where to begin."

"Well, did you have fun?" Todd asked.

"Yes . . . and no."

Mrs. Leighton looked puzzled. "Please explain, Lexi."

"Yesterday was great. We went on a long hike,

had a Bible study in the woods, and played softball. After supper we sang some songs and had devotions together. We had a neat lady for a chaperon. Her name is Emily. I think Pastor Lake has a crush on her."

"Oh-oh, romance . . ." Harry rubbed his hands together. "Tell us more, Lexi."

"There isn't any more to tell about them, really. We girls got to sleep around two *a.m.*"

"No wonder you look so tired," Mrs. Leighton said.

"It wasn't getting to sleep late that did it, Mom. It was getting up so early. Just before dawn, while I was having this crazy dream, the smoke alarm went off."

"Smoke alarm? Was there a fire?" Todd suddenly looked alert.

"More smoke than fire. The entire building was full of it. The power was out, and it was so weird and scary trying to get out of the building in the darkness, when we could hardly breathe. Pastor Lake and Emily helped us get out. Then they counted heads to make sure we were all there. That's when we discovered that Ruth was missing."

"Ruth? Who's Ruth?" Harry asked.

"Ruth Miller is a new girl at school," Todd explained. "Her parents are missionaries, and she lives with her aunt."

"Ruth is hearing-impaired," Lexi continued. "She didn't wake up like the rest of us because she couldn't hear anything. She wears hearing aids, but takes them out at night. I was supposed to wake her in the morning, but in all the confusion, I forgot about her."

Mrs. Leighton gasped. "Oh my, she could have died of smoke inhalation."

"I know. We all thought about that afterward. Pastor Lake went back inside for her, but it was tense for the seconds before he and Ruth emerged from the building." Lexi put her head in her hands. "It was awful . . . to think what could have happened."

"I guess it was a good thing I didn't go," Todd mused. "You would have had to rescue two of us. I'm not too speedy yet on these crutches."

"Oh, Todd," Lexi said, sitting down on the couch beside him. "I guess you're right. Anyway, when we got back to the church we spent some time discussing what happened. We all have a new appreciation for our sense of hearing, and for our lives."

"That sure was a close call," Harry commented.

"Yes, and it's strange, you know," Lexi said, "but being deaf never seemed like such a severe handicap to me. I suppose it's because it's not a visible thing. Someone who's blind, paralyzed, or mentally retarded is more obviously handicapped. Without her hearing aids, Ruth *looks* perfectly normal. It's easy to forget how cut off from the world she is without them."

Lexi paused, deep in thought. "Sometimes when I go to visit Grandma at the home, I get impatient with the other residents who can't hear very well. If I don't have much time, I don't stop by their rooms or wheelchairs because I know I'll have to yell into their ears or repeat myself half a dozen times. I'm never going to avoid them again. I know now that they need me to greet them as much as anyone else— maybe even more."

"Then, the retreat wasn't completely wasted," Harry reasoned.

"Wasted? Not at all. It was one of the most meaningful times I've ever spent. I feel I have more understanding and compassion than I did before. And I think most of those on the retreat will look at the disabled with new eyes."

"Sounds like you got your money's worth, Lexi," Todd said, placing an arm around her shoulder.

"Uh-huh. And you know what else, Harry Cramer?"

"Uh-oh, I sense a *Lexi lecture* coming on."

"You're the one who always loves to play music so loudly. You clamp the headset on and crank the volume."

"So?"

"Did you know that you can damage your hearing just by playing music too loudly?"

"Really? I didn't realize—"

"Well, now you know, so you'd better stop, okay? Because, when I lecture you, I want you to be able to hear me!"

Todd burst out laughing. "I guess she told you, huh, Cramer?"

"And *you*, Mr. Winston," Lexi continued in her lecturing tone. "The noise gets pretty loud at your brother's garage, too. It wouldn't be a bad idea to wear ear plugs when you're working around those engines. Besides, Mike always has the volume on the radio as high as it will go."

"I guess you're right. Some days I come home from the garage feeling like I'm wearing earmuffs."

Mrs. Leighton chuckled. Lexi had almost forgotten her mother was still standing in the doorway. "Now that Lexi has put you both in your place, I think I'll go back to the kitchen. Nice to have you home, Lexi. I'm glad you're all right."

"Thanks, Mom, but I think I do need a few hours' sleep."

Just then the doorbell rang, and Lexi peeked through the lace curtain at the living room window. "It's Egg and Binky! Quick, Harry, hide somewhere!"

Harry dived behind the wall separating the living room from the dining room. "Is this okay?"

"Fine. Stay put, now." Lexi went to the door. "Hi, guys. Come on in. Todd's here."

"Great! Egg and I were both so exhausted, all we wanted to do was sleep, but once we got home we were too wound up to do that," Binky chattered on. Her hair was disheveled and her glasses askew on her face. "I feel like I'm a bundle of nerves. I suppose I should have at least taken a shower, but—"

"Binky!" Harry sprang from his hiding place and gathered Binky into his arms.

She squealed with delight. "Harry Cramer! What are you doing here?" Binky pulled away from him and stood back to stare. She smoothed her hair with one hand, and tried to remove her glasses with the other.

"Wait a minute. What are you doing?" Harry held Binky's hands and looked into her eyes.

"I—uh . . ." Binky stammered. "I'm sorry I look so awful, Harry. Did Lexi tell you what happened? Why don't I just run home and freshen up . . ."

"Let me look at you," Harry insisted. "There's something different about you, but I don't know what it is."

Binky grimaced and squirmed, appalled that Harry had caught her with her glasses on before she could explain.

"I know they're pretty bad, but—"

"It's the glasses! They do things for you, Binky. They make you look older, even prettier."

"Older?" Egg squawked.

"Prettier?" Binky stopped squirming and looked up at Harry, dreamy-eyed. "Really? Do you mean it?"

"I wouldn't say it if I didn't mean it." Harry smiled with genuine appreciation.

Binky had to believe him. She beamed from ear to ear, and self-consciously smoothed her hair away from her face.

"Well, thank you. Of course, I kind of like them, too . . ."

"Can you believe it?" Lexi whispered to Todd.

"Maybe we won't hear so much about the glasses anymore," Todd answered.

Lexi giggled. "I predict Binky will take better care of them from now on. She probably won't break them for at least a month."

Her confidence buoyed by Harry's compliments, Binky rattled on excitedly about the fire at the retreat center, and about her new friend Ruth.

Todd reached for Lexi's hand and held it firmly. "I'm glad you came back early, Lexi."

"It's good to be home," Lexi agreed, smiling.

BOOK #17

There is something peculiar about the pretty new girl at Cedar River—why won't she let anyone near her? Lexi and her friends are suspicious, but Egg falls in love! Their shocking discovery about the girl makes them all think more seriously about what they have to be thankful for.

A Note From Judy

I'm glad you're reading *Cedar River Daydreams*! I hope I've given you something to think about as well as a story to entertain you. If you feel you have any of the problems that Lexi and her friends experience, I encourage you to talk with your parents, a pastor, or a trusted adult friend. There are many people who care about you!

Also, I enjoy hearing from my readers, so if you'd like to write, my address is:

Judy Baer
Bethany House Publishers
6820 Auto Club Road
Minneapolis, MN 55438

Please include an <u>addressed, stamped envelope</u> if you would like an answer. Thanks.